The

Gaius

DIARY

GENE EDWARDS

Tyndale House Publishers, Inc.
Wheaton, Illinois

Author's Note: The Day of Pentecost took place in A.D. 30. The burning of Rome took place on July 18, A.D. 64. The deaths of Paul, Nero, and Peter took place in A.D. 68. Jerusalem was destroyed in A.D. 70. The Flavian reign ended when the last Flavian, Domitian, died in A.D. 96. The emperor Nerva was reigning in A.D. 98.

Visit Tyndale's exciting Web site at www.tyndale.com

The Gaius Diary

Copyright © 2002 by Gene Edwards. All rights reserved.

Designed by Ron Kaufmann

Edited by MaryLynn Layman

Scripture quotations are taken from the *Holy Bible*, New Living Translation, copyright © 1996. Used by permission of Tyndale House Publishers, Inc., Wheaton, Illinois 60189. All rights reserved.

Library of Congress Cataloging-in-Publication Data
Edwards, Gene, date.
  The Gaius diary / by Gene Edwards.
    p. cm. — (First-century diaries)
  ISBN 0-8423-3871-3
    1. Church history—Primitive and early church, ca. 30-600—Ficiton.
2. Rome—History—Nero, 54-68—Fiction. 3. Peter, the Apostle, Saint—
Fiction. 4. Paul, the Apostle, Saint—Fiction. 5. Christian saints—
Fiction. 6. Apostles—Fiction. I. Title.
PS3555.D924 G35 2002
813'.54—dc21   2001007762

Printed in the United States of America

07 06 05 04 03 02
 8   7   6   5   4   3   2   1

*To my brother, in blood and in Christ, who has labored
for his Lord among American Indians in one of the most
remote villages in America, without fame or funds.
He will receive his reward in other realms.
To
Bill Edwards*

BOOKS BY GENE EDWARDS

First-Century Diaries
The Silas Diary
The Titus Diary
The Timothy Diary
The Priscilla Diary
The Gaius Diary

An Introduction to the Deeper Christian Life
The Highest Life
The Secret to the Christian Life
The Inward Journey

The Chronicles of the Door
The Beginning
The Escape
The Birth
The Triumph
The Return

Healing for the Inner Man
Crucified by Christians
A Tale of Three Kings
The Prisoner in the Third Cell
Letters to a Devastated Christian

In a Class by Itself
The Divine Romance

Radical Books
Revolution: The Story of the Early Church
Overlooked Christianity
Rethinking Elders
Beyond Radical
Climb the Highest Mountain

PROLOGUE

I, Gaius, have just received word that John has been banished to the island named Patmos.

The other eleven apostles are all dead.

Of the eight men Paul trained in Ephesus, only I am still alive.

Priscilla asked me to write the final chapters in the story, which began with Pentecost and ended with the destruction of Jerusalem. From the Day of Pentecost when the church was born to the destruction of Jerusalem is forty years!

For those of us who have survived beyond that last event, there followed a great persecution of the believers by Flavius Domitian, son of the emperor Flavius Vespasian.

Today, sixty-six years after Pentecost, only John and I, Gaius, are still alive.

As to these years, I trust you have read Priscilla's account of the first half of Paul's journey to Rome. It is now left to me to tell you the second half of the journey—about Paul's imprisonment in Rome, about the day he stood before Nero, and about Nero's madness and his attempt to destroy the faith. I will also chronicle for you the deaths of the Twelve, of Paul, and of the eight men who served beside Paul.

To take up the story where Priscilla left off, we find Paul being taken to Rome as a prisoner.

Because the journey began late in the sailing season, Paul

was apprehensive about the voyage. He feared the northeastern winds. If those winds struck early, the ship was doomed.

These dreaded winds, called the Etesian winds, *did* strike early. At the time these winds came the ship was on the south side of the island of Crete, at a point called Fair Havens. Because this town had no harbor, to remain there meant spending four months on board ship.

It was only forty miles to an excellent port near the Crete city of Phoenix. Paul was opposed to the attempt to reach Phoenix. He predicted destruction if the captain attempted to set sail. But to everyone else forty miles seemed a short and safe distance. They were to be proven wrong.

I, Gaius, shall take up the story exactly at that moment when the decision was made for the ship to depart Fair Havens and make a run for the seaport city of Phoenix.

CHAPTER 1

Only forty miles!"

The argument between the three men was long, and it was intense.

"We can almost see the Phoenix harbor from here. It is one of the best harbors on all the island of Crete," grumbled the ship's owner.

"But we are passing the last days before the Etesian winds," retorted Julius, the captain of the guards, the man responsible for the two hundred prisoners on board. "Do you understand that according to the ancient ways of the Romans, if even one prisoner escapes, the officer in charge is killed? *I* am that officer."

"If we do not make it," said the captain of the ship, "you will not have to worry about having your head severed. We will all be at the bottom of the sea. There is little hope for any ship that is not harbored when those winds hit. On the other hand, sir, forty miles is not far! We can make it in less than a day."

"If!" snapped the Roman captain.

The ship's owner continued his argument: "If we stay here at Fair Havens, we will be aboard this ship for the next four months, *if* we survive! Four months for over two hundred prisoners, *and* my crew, not moving a single foot. It would be the most miserable life imaginable. Your prisoners will almost certainly revolt, and the sailors may very well mutiny."

"And your wheat would rot," responded Julius dryly, then added, "I desire that you listen to one of my prisoners. Think not of him as a criminal. He is a man of God. I have found it wise to listen to this man."

Julius presented Paul to the owner and the captain. "This is Paul of Tarsus, who, according to the letter that I have with me, has been falsely charged and will almost certainly be acquitted when he stands before Nero. Speak, Paul."

The sea captain sniffed. The ship's owner turned away in dismay.

"I am certain," said Paul slowly, "if you try to reach the harbor of Phoenix, you will be setting a course for destruction. This ship will be lost—your cargo and also the crew, the prisoners, and the passengers." Paul's words sounded as though they had been dipped in doom.

"Now I am being asked to follow the wishes of a religious madman and criminal," said the ship's owner.

"In the end it is your decision," the captain said, deferring to Julius. "Roman law placed you in charge of this ship the moment you stepped aboard."

Julius's eyes shifted back and forth. "Forty miles," he replied. "You can make it in a day?"

"*If* the winds are with us."

"Are the winds with you right now?"

"Yes. They are good winds, and they are warm ones. If these winds hold, we will make it safely."

"Then hoist sails and move."

Paul glared at the ship's owner. "You are now a man devoid of one ship."

Moments later the ship plied the waters of a smooth sea in what seemed to be an almost certain drive to the next harbor.

"Why, Paul?" asked Aristarchus, who had heard everything Paul had said.

"Why, what?" responded Paul.

"Why are you so certain of impending disaster? How do you know?"

"I have never been able to answer that question," said Paul. "I simply know. It comes from listening to the Lord's voice . . . within."

Aristarchus took a deep breath, shook his head, and walked away.

"We are on the southern side of Crete. Does not the land itself give us some protection from bad winds?" asked Aristarchus as he turned back toward Paul.

"If the northeasters begin to blow, nothing—absolutely nothing—will be safe. From where we are now, if the winds change and blow upon us from the northeast, we will be driven southwest. Do you know what lies southwest of us?"

Aristarchus turned the question over in his mind. "Egypt."

"The *shoals* of Egypt. These shoals have taken more ships to the bottom of the sea than has any other place in all the world! There is no land between here and that graveyard. *That* is where we will end up."

A few hours later Aristarchus sensed the winds were beginning to change.

"The Etesian winds," said Paul. "I can smell them. I can feel them. I consider those winds my mortal enemy. They have tried to take me more than once. Long ago an ancient sailor on the island of Cyprus gave me a word of warning: 'Never sail the Etesian winds.' And now, here I am, coming to the end of my life. . . ."

"Do not talk that way," said Aristarchus.

"I am sorry, Aristarchus, but men who are in their sixties do not live much longer, no matter how good their health. As I was about to say, I stand in the latter days of my life, once more fac-

ing these horrid winds. Whether they crush us against the rocks
or turn the ship upside down, neither you nor I nor any other
mother's son will ever see home again."

(Paul's last words were a quotation of an ancient saying
among sailors when they perceived that their voyage was
headed for calamity.)

"In a few hours this ship will be at the mercy of God.
Where is Luke?" asked Paul.

"He is right where you always find him. He is at the front of
the ship watching everything. I have never seen a man of the
land so obsessed with the sea," chuckled Aristarchus.

It was October the tenth.

One man wanted his grain to get sold in the marketplaces
of Rome. Another wanted to be a good captain of a ship. Another had risked his very neck in order to secure a safe harbor.
Another predicted total ruin.

Paul glanced up at Mount Ida, the highest point on
Crete. "This may be the last time we will ever see sunlight," he
mused.

"It is coming, and it will be a typhonic," muttered Luke as
he greeted Paul.

A soaking rain began, the coast blurring under its cloak.
The sun disappeared in dark clouds.

"Sails will not take this for very long," said Paul grimly.

"Interestingly, I have no idea whether we should go below
or stay here. This ship may sink very fast."

At that moment the captain stepped to Paul's side. "It is a
levanter. I will never be able to hold the ship against these
winds. All we can do is lower the sails and pray to whatever gods
there be."

"Can we make the island of Cauda?" asked Luke.

"There is a tiny port at Cauda but nothing that would help
us now, nor is there any way to navigate into its port," answered
the distraught captain.

The captain walked away, calling to the sailors, "Pull up the dinghy. It is filled with water."

Luke immediately joined the sailors. A few minutes later he reappeared. "That was not an easy task."

"What are they doing now, Luke?" asked Aristarchus.

The answer froze the blood in his veins.

The sailors are about to wrap the entire ship with rope, from one end of the hull to the other. Then they will tighten the ropes in hopes that the coming waves will not bash this old freighter to pieces."

"It is that bad?" questioned shivering Aristarchus.

"Worse," replied Luke. "Tying rope around a ship has rarely ever helped anything."

"What is actually going to sink us?" asked a resolved Aristarchus.

"The timber could rip to pieces," responded Luke, "or a leak could break out under the waterline. The ship would become waterlogged and sink. We could be driven on some rocks. Foundering, though, is our most likely fate."

"Foundering?"

"Sinking right out here in the middle of nowhere."

"Look over there—the sailors are lowering the masts," said Paul with a wide motion. "The sails are coming down."

"Now all we have to fear is north Africa," laughed Luke. It is actually called the Gulf of Syrtis Major. "Hmmm," he added, "I think I know what they are about to do."

Agitated, soaked to the skin, cold, and dripping wet, Aristarchus asked, "How do you know all this? You are a doctor, not a sailor."

"By asking questions," replied a bemused Luke. "Next the sailors will probably try to turn the ship at an angle, so that the front of the ship, not the side, will catch the winds. That might slow her down a bit."

Luke turned to Paul and said helplessly, "Paul, I believe we should get below."

The three men descended into the belly of the ship. Doom was on the face of every man down there.

In the lantern light, Paul looked around. "So much wheat."

"And so much water. This is not good," added Luke.

"What do you mean?" asked Aristarchus again.

"This storm has a friend as destructive as the storm itself." Paul pointed to a specific portion of the cargo.

"See those jars?" Luke said. "They are called *amphorae* and hold grain. Each one is three feet tall and about eighteen inches wide. Probably they were made on the island of Rhodes. These are very cheap jars. The clay is porous. Water can seep through the clay and go right to the grain. When this ship begins to settle deeper in the sea, the water will reach the grain. Wet grain swells ten times its original size, which means the ship will get much heavier. Beyond that, some of the jars will explode. Consider this and the fact that there are a thousand of these jars on board. *This* will help sink the ship as much as the storm will."

Luke had managed to smile all the time he was telling Aristarchus this news.

"Then we are *surely* going to sink!" exclaimed Aristarchus.

"Exactly," replied Luke. "One more nice piece of news. Have you noticed this ship has already begun to list?"

Each sunless day thereafter the ship did sink just a little deeper into the sea.

What no one knew was that the ship was also being moved by the winds about one and a half miles an hour westward. That unknown fact would keep them from the Gulf of Syrtis

Major. What good would that do? None, if in the end the ship were to sink.

On the twelfth day of the storm, the crew gave up all hope of being saved. The ship had sunk too deep in the water to survive. Foundering was inevitable, whether the storm continued or miraculously ended. Furthermore, if every man on board dropped into the sea ever so cautiously, even then every soul would die. Yet on that same hopeless morning Paul burst out upon the stormy deck with this proclamation: "There is a way! Where is the captain?" he asked as he disappeared into the dark.

When Paul found the captain, the owner, and Julius, his words sounded like those of a deranged madman.

"Men, you should have listened to me in the first place and not left Fair Havens. You would have avoided all this injury and loss. But take courage! None of you will lose your lives, even though the ship will go down."

"And how do you know all this?" grumbled the seasick owner.

"Last night an angel of the God to whom I belong and whom I serve stood beside me, and he said, 'Don't be afraid, Paul, for you will surely stand trial before Caesar! What's more, God in his goodness has granted safety to everyone sailing with you.' So take courage! For I believe God. It will be just as he said. But we will be shipwrecked on an island."

For the first time, both the captain of the ship and the ship's owner took Paul's words seriously. The captain glanced at Julius. Julius nodded.

"Well," said the captain, sighing, "I have no choice but to obey you. Either way we die. This ship has only a few hours before it goes under." The captain then ordered four anchors to be moved from the front to the rear of the ship.

"A wise move. This may keep us from the rocks," shouted Paul above the roar of the sea.

"What rocks? Where? When?" asked the captain.

"I do not know," called Paul, "but soon. Let us pray for light."

"Prayer is all we have," said Luke as he stuck his head out of the bowels of the ship and stared into the blackness. "The water prohibits our staying down here beyond this instant."

At that very moment, a plot was brewing among the sailors to abandon not only the ship but the passengers, the captain, and the prisoners.

The plan was simple: "Let us pretend we are dropping anchor, but instead we will lower the dinghy, plunge into the sea, and then haul ourselves to the dinghy . . . and row!"

"What are those men doing?" cried Paul, even as the mutineers were about to drop the dinghy into the sea.

"They *should* be lowering an anchor," replied the captain, "but they are not." Instantly Julius barked an order to his soldiers.

"You will all die unless the sailors stay aboard," added Paul.

Awkwardly the soldiers made their way to the rear of the tossing ship. There, hesitantly and then bravely, they cut away the lifeboat. The dinghy fell into the sea. A moment later it drifted out into the darkness. The subdued sailors stepped back from the points of Roman swords.

"Captain! Julius!" Paul then motioned to some of the soldiers and sailors to approach him.

"For fourteen days we have not eaten. You are all hungry and you are weak." Paul then turned to Julius and to the ship's captain. "I beg you. No, I implore you, everyone . . . please eat something. Your life depends on it. Every man here will need all the strength of his being in the next few hours. Do as I say, and no one will be lost in this sea." Paul then lifted a piece of bread into the air and, in a loud voice, offered thanks to God. With deliberation he began to eat.

A few moments later food protected in jars was passed

around, and 276 souls followed suit. No one seemed to notice that Paul was now in charge.

"Dump the rest of the cargo!" directed Paul with a loud voice. "We all know the ship is doomed, but it is sinking too fast. Empty it."

The captain nodded. So did the ship's owner. "Life is more important than grain and wood," he commented philosophically.

Even as the last of the grain fell into the sea, someone cried, "Daylight!" It was in truth the first sight of light in two weeks. In a moment everyone was on deck straining into the lifting darkness.

"Look! Land! It is a bay. But where?"

"I know this sea from one end to the other, and I have never seen this place before," a sailor called out.

"We will be dashed upon the shores at any moment. See . . . rocks over there!" called the captain.

"Yes, but I see a sandy beach over there!" roared Luke.

"Cut away the anchors!" cried the captain frantically. "We hope and we pray that we drift into that sandy beach. Our souls are now in the hands of the gods."

"How far away is that beach, Luke?" asked a not-so-calm Aristarchus.

"Perhaps a half mile," guessed Luke.

"It is interesting to stand here and watch yourself about to live or die, depending on a drifting, anchorless ship," whispered Aristarchus.

"If she beaches, we will be able to virtually walk ashore . . . but if we hit the rocks . . . !"

What everyone was seeing was actually a small piece of land jutting out from the island's mainland. Between the ship and that tiny piece of beach was a swift crosscurrent of water the local people called "where two seas meet."

Every soul stood breathless as they watched the ship

approach the shore. Then came a strong jerk of the ship. There she stuck as she ran aground, unable to move.

"She is buried in mud," declared one of the sailors. "As she tosses about she will be ripped to shreds."

"She will splinter into a thousand pieces," observed a watchful Paul.

The soldiers, by the instinct of years of training, were taking their places to kill as many prisoners as possible.

"Why?" cried Luke. "Why are they about to commit such an atrocity?"

"Roman justice!" replied Paul.

"Some will escape," explained the ship's owner, "and if anyone does, that means death for every soldier on this ship."

What was going through the mind of Julius in that moment of finality?

Am I willing to save Paul and in so doing risk having my own head chopped off? Surely some of these prisoners will escape.

Turning to Julius, one of the soldiers called out, "Shall we kill them?"

Paul lunged toward Julius to implore him to spare the prisoners, but Julius gave his order. "No," he cried. "Let them live! When you reach shore, try to form a crescent around the bay." Then, above the screams of the sea Julius bellowed, "Now, everyone into the sea, but no one goes until the soldiers have!"

A moment later the crew and the prisoners followed the soldiers into the boiling sea. Some swam, some paddled to shore on boards and planks, and others instantly learned to swim.

Paul was one of the last to leave the almost totally destroyed ship.

The island Paul was about to set foot on would hold for him a unique experience. The four months Paul would be on this island would mark the most successful period of his ministry.

That success had its beginning with a poisonous snake and the healing of the sick father of a very powerful man.

Paul knew nothing of this as he braced himself to leave the ship and enter the savage waters.

Paul caught his breath as he slipped into the churning water.

Bitter cold, he thought. For a moment he treaded water, looking back at the ship, then forward at the human cargo struggling to reach shore.

I once told the Corinthians I had been shipwrecked three times. That is wrong; now it is four, he thought as he pushed toward the beach.

Paul's first shipwreck had been the most brutal. This one, though, followed two long, cold weeks. For fourteen days and nights 276 souls had not seen the sun nor eaten one bite of food. In that first shipwreck Paul found shelter on board a ship that plucked him out of the sea. Here, there was no rescuing ship, no shelter, *nothing*. Winter's blast appeared to be the only welcome these men would receive.

Suddenly a mysterious fire appeared on shore. A large fire it was, enough to warm nearly three hundred castaways.

As Paul dragged himself up on the beach, he looked around for Luke and Aristarchus. The fire was bright enough to reveal them, but he did not see them.

They are here somewhere—I know it.

Paul slipped as close to the fire as he dared. All around there were smiling faces that did not belong to anyone from the ship. People of the island had come and started this fire.

"You are kind to think of us," said Paul, first in Greek, then in Latin. "Your fire may save our lives." The only response was smiles and nods. *Most of these people don't speak either Greek or Latin. Where are we?* he wondered.

"We are on the island of Malta. This island is just south of Sicily. We are south and west of the city of Syracuse, Sicily. Someone who speaks Greek just informed me," said Julius.

"Malta?" said Paul. "I thought we were near Egypt."

"The gods have been good to you," replied Julius as he handed Paul some food. "Water, fresh water, will be here soon."

Paul turned to the people standing nearby and began saying thank you in every language and dialect he knew. *They understand nothing I say.* Paul then turned back to Julius. "You have divested yourself of your uniform."

"Either that or drown," said Julius with a shrug.

Someone on the crowded beach, seeing the two men so amicable, asked in Latin, "Is he not one of your prisoners?"

"He is my friend," replied Julius.

Paul laughed as he held up the shackles around his wrist. "It is possible for a prisoner to be a friend of his captor, especially if both are Roman citizens."

The questioner laughed nervously and slipped away.

Later Paul spied Aristarchus. For a moment Paul feared he had another John Mark on his hands, as Aristarchus was coughing, and he was very pale. But the first words out of Aristarchus's mouth dispelled such a notion. "Greetings, Brother Paul. Now I have a shipwreck story of my own to tell!"

The two men grabbed one another and rejoiced to their Lord with great relief.

"Where is Luke?" queried Paul.

"I have no idea. Like the rest of us, I have a notion that these incredible people sought him out, gave him some bread and water, and by now have discovered he is a doctor. Paul, who are these people?"

"We are on an island called Malta. It is just below Sicily. In all my days I do not think I have ever met so kind and gentle a people." (Nor were his words inaccurate.)

"I have a notion they may be used to coming out here and saving people from the sea," observed Aristarchus. "Surely ours is not the first ship ever to be driven upon these shores. But Sicily. I thought we were supposed to die on the shoals of Egypt!"

"At some point in the last few days, the wind must have changed. We were pushed from south to west. To this we owe our lives."

Paul and Aristarchus began circling the large fire, surveying every face. As expected, the two men found Luke tending to the wounds of one of the prisoners.

"The beloved physician," murmured Paul.

"The incomparable physician," responded Aristarchus admiringly.

While the three men were speaking, Julius appeared again.

"You have made it, *all three!*"

"And the rest of the passengers?" asked Paul.

"I have no idea. But at this point, I would say virtually everyone is here. Possibly all. Now take a moment to look out to the sea."

The three men looked. The ship was in the last moments of its death throes. No more than a minute later, its hull crumbled and sank into the sea.

"Now it is driftwood," said Julius quietly.

"And the owner?" asked Aristarchus.

"Well, you will not believe this, but he has taken it all in stride. I think he is simply glad to be alive. Nonetheless, he knows that he has entered the ranks of the poor."

"Aristarchus, while Luke attends the injured, let's gather some wood," said Paul. "You don't mind, do you, Julius? We will not wander far from this encampment."

Julius nodded. He then signaled to one of the soldiers to

join them. "Accompany these men. One is free. Treat the other as free, for *he* is responsible for saving your life!"

In the woods, the two men found a great deal of loose brush, sticks, and branches. Bundling the wood into two piles, they returned to the fire. Paul slipped to his knees and began throwing the wood onto the fire, piece by piece. Suddenly the head of a poisonous snake shot up out of the bundle of wood. In an instant it had buried its fangs into Paul's hand. He stood up, inched his way closer to the fire, and shook off the snake into the blaze.

"He is a prisoner, is he not?" asked one of the Maltese.

"Of sorts," responded Aristarchus.

"Then the gods must have known he was a murderer. They are rendering justice to him. This man will now swell up and die."

For a long time there was total silence around Paul, even as he continued to toss branches into the fire.

"Only a few minutes more," said one.

Julius also watched. Even some of the soldiers moved in beside Julius to stare. As word of the snake passed to everyone around the fire, a crowd gathered to watch Paul die.

"He should be dead by now," said someone in a loud voice.

"It will come. The gods have their ways," said another.

Soon, nearly everyone on the beach had encircled Paul. Paul, playing his role to the hilt, continued throwing branches onto the fire.

"That is no man," someone said softly. "The poisonous snake has buried its venom into him, yet he does not die! That cannot be."

"Then surely he is a god!"

The people began backing away. Luke and Aristarchus were savoring every moment. It was the telling moment of the entire journey—for passengers, for prisoners, for guards, and for the people of Malta. Everyone knew now that truly this was either a god or a man of God.

"You have made quite an impression here," said Julius, shaking his head in wonder.

"Oh?" said Paul coolly.

The people began motioning to Paul to follow them. "Shall I?" asked Paul.

"By all means. I think they want you to enter the city, which, I am told, is nearby. They call it Valletta."

Aristarchus finally began meeting people whose language he could understand. "They speak Latin! Should this not be part of the Greek world?"

"It appears Romans have turned the people of Malta into good Italians," jested Julius. "I have sent a band of my soldiers into the city with Paul to let the officials there know that I am expecting them to find a safe place for my soldiers and prisoners—and a *special* place for Paul. We owe him much.

"As far as we can tell, every soul who was on that ship made it safely to shore. Every prisoner is under the blade. I remind you, had even one prisoner escaped, I would have been beheaded, and so also my soldiers. As it is, I will almost certainly be hailed as a hero. I can hear it now: 'The gods are with Julius!' It would be more to the truth if they were to say: 'Paul's God is with Julius.' I will see to it that this city gives its best to Paul."

The moment was broken by the appearance of one of Julius's soldiers.

"Captain, it is most remarkable. I have just been informed that the chief magistrate of this island is a man named Publius, and we landed on *his* estate!"

Julius shook his head. "Amazing! Find him. Tell him our situation. He may believe you. Take some of your fellow soldiers with you."

By late afternoon 276 men had come safely into the city of Valletta. That evening Julius rented a house for himself *and* Paul.

Late that night Julius came into Paul's room, pulled off his helmet, and dropped his sword beside him.

"I have met Publius. Perhaps you would be interested in this. His father is at the point of death. Forgive me, but I told him of you. He has requested that you come and pray for his father, in the name of this unique God of yours."

As I, Gaius, have said, what followed is the most successful preaching of the gospel that Paul of Tarsus ever experienced.

That very night Paul went to Publius's mansion, and there he prayed for Publius's father, who had dysentery and fever. Having prayed for the elderly man, Paul then laid hands on him. Remarkably, the man was instantly healed.

By noon the next day there were people pouring into Valletta from nearby towns and villages to be healed. By the following day people were coming from all over the island. All this was taking place at no less than the governor's villa. It was not long before Paul, given full freedom of the island, was preaching the gospel in Valletta, and later across the island. Word of this man's coming reached almost every ear on the island.

By late winter there were proportionately more people confessing Jesus Christ as Savior on that island than any other place Paul had ever set foot.

Perhaps I should now inform you that at the time when Paul was on Malta, he had fewer than eight years left to live. Aristarchus had only four years to live. It had been only thirty years since Pentecost in Jerusalem. But in just ten years there would come the total destruction of Jerusalem and its temple.

Then came February. As winter began coming to a close, Julius conscripted an Alexandrian grain ship bound for Rome to take on his prisoners and soldiers. It was a large ship. Under her prow were carved the two figures of the twin gods, Castor and Pollux.

Although the winter had not quite ended, the captain of

that ship had seen a break in the winter weather. He decided to take advantage of it and sail on to the next good harbor.

It was not long before Paul, Luke, and Aristarchus stood on deck, staring up at the great volcano Vesuvius. In its shadow was the city of Pompeii. As they sailed past Pompeii they could not have imagined that the sleeping Vesuvius would erupt just nineteen years later and bury Pompeii forever.

To their relief, good weather continued to offer its graces, which gave the three men time to recover from their ordeal.

"We will make Puteoli," said the captain with certainty. "Ours will be one of the first ships to dock in this new season. That means the grain will bring a premium price.

"Have you ever seen Puteoli?" he asked.

"No," said Luke. "I have never seen Italy, and I have certainly never seen Rome."

"Puteoli is the chief port of the west side of Italy. You will see many ships docked there, probably more than anywhere on earth. Some ships will be grain ships, but most will be military."

As the ship pulled into the Puteoli harbor, Julius reluctantly put Paul back in fetters.

"It is for my superiors. They must see every man in chains. But I will tell them of you. I swear by the gods that I will protect you, and furthermore I will see to it that you have a private escort into Rome."

"You have been gracious, Julius," replied Paul.

"How far is Rome from the Puteoli port?" asked Aristarchus.

"Rome is over fifty miles inland. We will be taking a very famous and ancient road called the Appian Way."

The three men fell silent. The very term the *Appian Way* was almost mythic, for it was the greatest of all the roads of the Roman Empire, a road built to last a thousand years.

Shortly thereafter the ship docked. Never had anyone seen so many ships. Some were Roman battleships, a few were passenger ships capable of carrying hundreds in comfort, the rest were mostly freighters.

The prisoners, except Paul, were chained together and marched off to Rome. Paul was also chained, but he was being accompanied by a small contingent of Roman guards.

You would not be surprised to learn that from the moment he set foot on Puteoli soil, Paul plied everyone he met with questions.

"Are there any Jews back in Rome since Nero has come to the throne?"

"Yes, a few have just recently begun to return."

"Have there been any problems?"

"No. Nero is ignoring Claudius's decree."

"No Jew has been arrested, hurt, or killed?"

"None."

At his own expense, Luke sent a courier to Rome. Whether or not the message would actually reach Priscilla and Aquila, they could not know. After all, even the smartest of couriers could not always find his way around *that* city, for not a single street was marked or named. Beyond that, some couriers simply took the money given for their services and were never heard of again. Nonetheless, the three men held out some hope that the assembly in Rome would know of Paul's safe arrival in Italy.

Even while still in Puteoli, Paul sent off letters to Antioch and to Ephesus, telling of his safe arrival and asking that all the men he had trained in Ephesus come immediately to Rome.

In each letter he wrote one sentence common to all: "Make sure that Epaphras has heard. Send him to me if at all possible."

I, Gaius, was the only one of those whom Paul trained who did not receive a letter about his safe arrival. I was, after all, in northern Egypt, and no one knew my exact location. Nonetheless, word eventually reached me. At that time I knew my place was in north Africa. The decision to stay in Egypt may have saved my life, as you will soon see.

Having left Puteoli, Paul and his company journeyed some forty-three miles and reached a place called Appii Forum. Because Paul was exhausted, he asked to remain there a few days. And why not? Paul was no longer a young man nor even a middle-aged man. (He later referred to himself as "Paul the ancient," which is exactly what he was.)

The soldiers agreed to let Paul rest at Appii Forum for one or two days. All along the way, Paul, Luke, and Aristarchus had watched the faces of people passing them on the road, hoping that Paul's letter to Priscilla had arrived safely and that a messenger might have been sent to meet them. Nonetheless, if someone had been sent, there would be only a slight chance of their actually meeting. It is not easy for people to search for and find sojourners, as there are too many taverns, too many inns, too many streets to guarantee success.

Near Appii Forum was a place called Tres Tabernae (Three Taverns). There they spotted a man running toward them. He, in turn, eyed the soldiers and their prisoner, turned around, and ran back up the road. An odd occurrence!

What Paul did not know was that the entire assembly from Rome had decided to come out to meet him! From the start, someone was always out in front, looking for Paul and his companions.

A few minutes later Paul heard singing. Everyone in Paul's party stopped . . . both soldiers and believers. Singing! That in itself was strange to the ears of the soldiers. Life was too hard for most people to ever sing.

"It is our brothers and sisters," said Paul, ever so softly. Aristarchus dropped to his knees and repeated, "It is our brothers and sisters, at last."

In a moment they appeared. "It's the whole ecclesia. All of them!" said Paul in sheer wonder. A moment later the pilgrims from Rome broke into a run. All headed straight for Paul.

As Paul was encircled, the soldiers stepped back. Those

who could not reach him were kissing and hugging Luke and Aristarchus. In the midst of the melee Priscilla appeared, then Aquila. Paul reached out and, taking Priscilla in his arms, began to shake. Weeping, he then turned and grasped Aquila. No one *ever* wanted to see that man cry. When Paul cried it was like Mount Vesuvius. Paul, now in Aquila's arms, erupted into long, convulsive sobs even as he shook like an earthquake.

Everyone in the crowd reached out to Paul, singing to him, praying for him, and exhorting him. Even some of the guards began to weep at such an unbelievable sight. They had never seen an expression of love such as this.

And so it was, as Luke later so beautifully put it, "We began to take a little courage." Paul of Tarsus had come at last to Rome. In the meantime the letters he had written and sent out from Puteoli spread across the empire and were causing quite a stir among the churches.

Especially that one sentence Paul had included in *all* his letters.

CHAPTER 4

Epaphras held up about twenty letters. "In the last few weeks I have received letters from *everywhere*—all of them telling me that Paul wants me to come to Rome, immediately."

Everyone in the Colosse assembly broke out in cheers.

"*Today* I received a letter from the assembly in Philippi up in Greece. The brothers and sisters *there* also heard from Paul, and even in his letter to them he was mentioning *me*. He told the assembly in Philippi to write me. They told me Paul wants me to go to Rome by way of Philippi. Then I am to report to him not only about Colosse but also Philippi and all of northern Greece."

Standing straight as an arrow, like the soldier he was, Epaphras asked innocently, "Shall I go?"

The brothers and sisters burst out laughing. "Do you have a choice?" asked one. "Of course you will," said another.

Epaphras hesitated.

"But I do not know how to get to Greece. I have never traveled beyond Ephesus. I do not even know where Greece is. And I surely do not know how to get to Rome."

"Go to Ephesus, and board a ship bound for Philippi. When you arrive there the brothers and sisters will show you how to get from Greece to Italy and then into Rome," said Philemon.

"Do they charge money for being on a ship?"

Again, everyone laughed. Epaphras was the most single-minded man *anyone* had ever known. He was interested in Christ and the gospel of Christ, and in planting the ecclesia. Nothing else interested him.

"We will see that your travels to Greece cost you *nothing*," assured everyone.

Epaphras, looking a little stunned, said resolutely, "Then I shall do as Paul desires." Those in the room who had traveled began sharing with him the ways, wonders, and woes of travel in the empire.

A few days later the Colossian assembly met in Philemon's home to bid farewell to their beloved Epaphras. Brothers and sisters from Laodicea and Hierapolis came to Colosse to join in the farewell. (Epaphras had raised up not only the church in Colosse but the assembly in Hierapolis and Laodicea.)

After fervent prayer and much beautiful singing, as only the Colossians could sing, Epaphras set out on foot for the ninety-mile journey to Ephesus.

What Epaphras did not know was that someone was following him. A runaway who had recently been whipped by his owner had stolen some money from him and determined to get as far away from Asia Minor as possible. In so doing he risked being branded on his face and possibly put to death. Hiding in the woods, always near, yet at a safe distance from Epaphras, this blond-haired, blue-eyed, white-skinned slave kept his features cloaked by a robe and hood. The young man, now about twenty-five, shadowed every step Epaphras made.

Who was this young man? Where would he flee? And what would be his ultimate fate?

CHAPTER 5

The assembly in Ephesus received Epaphras wildly for he was well remembered for the year he lived there, when he, along with the Eight, was trained by Paul. In fact, Epaphras was nearly a legend among the Ephesian Christians. They not only loved him dearly but cheered when they heard with what power he preached the gospel in eastern Asia Minor. Now they overflowed with joy that he was going to see Paul.

The very evening he arrived, the ecclesia in Ephesus came together to hear his report. Epaphras did not disappoint them. In his simple, straightforward way he proclaimed Christ to them so masterfully that everyone knew "this man has no peers."

It seems our brother Epaphras could cause the Lord's people to convulse with laughter yet never once notice that he did so. Even until this day not one of us knows if he was deliberately humorous or if he was utterly naïve about his own abilities. That was Epaphras! Once you met him you could not but love him.

On the day Epaphras sailed for the Greek city of Philippi, the Ephesian port was packed with believers to see him on his way, not only to Greece but also to Rome.

The ship eased its way out into the murky water of the

silted harbor of Ephesus, with no one aware that there was a barbarian stowaway.

On the second day out, while doing their rounds, the sailors accidentally discovered their stowaway. The other passengers, including Epaphras, heard of the discovery. One said, "He will be whipped within an inch of his life then left in the hold without food to die."

When the German slave was dragged toward the mast, Epaphras turned away. Then suddenly he said to himself, *I know that frame. Who is that?* Epaphras whirled around only to see a terrified young man being tied hand and foot to the mast, pleading in a deep, guttural language for mercy.

"Onesimus!"

The slave tried to turn himself but could not, but he recognized the resonating voice.

"Epaphras, save me! Save me!"

"Hold!" ordered Epaphras. And even at sea, among hard-bitten sailors, his words were instantly obeyed.

Epaphras ran to Onesimus's side. The youth once again begged for mercy. Epaphras instinctively knew what to do. (It was wisdom only God could give.)

"You wish to be saved, Onesimus?"

Still in tears Onesimus cried out. "Oh, please, please. Save me!"

"And how shall you be saved?"

The entire crew and passengers stood spellbound at this very strange encounter.

"Save me, Epaphras. *Please*, save me."

"Have you been in our meetings, Onesimus?"

"Yes! Please save me! Please!"

"I cannot save you, Onesimus. You know that."

Onesimus, still horrified, pulled his face across the splintering mast, trying in vain to see Epaphras's face.

"Epaphras, please."

"*I* cannot save you," whispered Epaphras.

Onesimus's face contorted in fear and confusion.

"There's only One who can save you."

Onesimus looked stunned. For a long moment Onesimus squeezed his eyes closed, then spoke. "Can the Lord? Can he really?"

"He can. But you are going to have to stop being so stubborn—stubborn just to *make* Philemon angry. And you must lay down your bitterness for being caught and enslaved. *Then* you believe!"

Onesimus's eyes dashed about wildly.

"I will. I do. I will. I do."

"Cut him down! I will pay his passage," said Epaphras matter-of-factly.

"It is double pay for a stowaway."

"The debt is paid."

Onesimus's body fell to the deck. He lay there, holding fast to Epaphras's feet and crying.

"He is a slave. See the brand, see the white hand. He should die."

"This is of no concern of yours," said Epaphras. "I know his master. He is forgiving."

Just what was Epaphras going to do with a runaway slave? As the ship entered the Philippian harbor, Epaphras knew he had to go to Rome, immediately. But just what could he do with this slave? The answer would have to come forth quickly.

CHAPTER 6

It was with total awe that Epaphras walked from the Philippian seaport into the city of Philippi. Never had he seen so many statues. Never had he seen so much marble. And everyone around him was speaking a language he did not understand. Onesimus, at his side, was even more impressed than Epaphras. When they reached the home of Lydia, Epaphras handed her a letter from the three churches in eastern Asia Minor. Lydia, never one to show surprise, nonetheless kept staring at Onesimus. "You, Epaphras, have a slave?"

"Not exactly."

"These letters are from churches in Asia Minor."

"Yes, the letters are to introduce me to the Philippian believers."

"Introduce Epaphras! You are a legend to us here! Paul wants you to stay here for a time to strengthen us before you go on to Rome."

"May I meet with some wise brothers and sisters? I have an immediate decision that must be made," responded Epaphras as he glanced at Onesimus.

Lydia smiled. "A rather *large* problem is he not?"

(Epaphras soon found himself being called *Epaphroditus,*

for that was his name in the Latin language. At first Epaphras was very uncomfortable with this name, as it sounded even more heathen than *Epaphras*. Nonetheless, he eventually settled into this new name and ultimately came to even enjoy it.)

What happened between Epaphras and the assembly in Philippi, as they came to know him, was wonderful but not unexpected. Like all the rest of us, the brothers and sisters in Philippi fell in love with him. Epaphras, a tall, raw-boned man who virtually never said anything except when he spoke of Christ, could easily give one the impression of being ignorant. That is, until he opened his mouth to speak.

And speak he did, to the assembly that gathered in Lydia's home. I, Gaius, am told he spoke for nearly *three* hours. No one moved, as each was absolutely enchanted. No one had ever spoken as did Epaphras . . . that is, *Epaphroditus*.

Very humbly, Epaphras sat down, crossed his legs, and put his elbows on his knees. The brothers and sisters, on the other hand, gathered around him, pulled him up, put their hands on him, and hugged and kissed him.

After the meeting Epaphras met with about fifteen people. There he introduced Onesimus. "He's a runaway!" said Epaphras. "I need your counsel."

"A runaway," echoed everyone in the room. Few people had *ever* seen a runaway slave. Slaves did *not* run away, and if they did, they died.

"Yes, I am a runaway," said Onesimus, his head down.

"Your master?"

"Philemon of Colosse."

"A believer?"

"I think so. He says he is."

"Onesimus," responded Epaphras sternly.

"He is. I just do not like him. I was born free."

"You would not like any man who took away that freedom, Onesimus," scolded Epaphras.

"Brothers, Philemon is a good master. Proud, yes, from a proud family. But not cruel."

"He worked me too hard!" broke in Onesimus.

"Is that worth dying a terrible death?"

"No," said Onesimus as he began to cry.

"Epaphras, what will happen if you send Onesimus back to Philemon now?" asked a sister.

"I have no idea. A beating? A branding? Death? I do not know."

A brother spoke. "Let us wait a few days before a decision is made."

"Please, yes, please," implored Onesimus.

The fate of Onesimus now lay in the hands of the assembly of Jesus Christ gathering in Philippi.

In the assembly there was one person every believer who came through Philippi wanted to meet. Epaphroditus was no exception. The jailer!

One early morning the jailer took Epaphras and Onesimus to the side of a stone hill where Paul and Silas had been imprisoned. There they stood at the door carved into the rock face, and there they stuck their heads into the large dark room where Paul and Silas had been shackled, their feet in wood stocks and their hands fettered in chains fastened deep inside the stone.

Both men were *very* impressed—as we all have been.

Lydia, in turn, brought Epaphras to the river, where Paul had proclaimed Christ to a small group of women.

Wherever Epaphras went, an ever-maturing Onesimus was always at his side.

Still, the question remained: What to do with Onesimus? Send him home? Ask Philemon to come to Greece to bring his slave back to Colosse, knowing he might order his death right there in Philippi? (The general opinion was that Philemon would not have Onesimus killed, not in the presence of the body of Christ. Onesimus, on the other hand, was not at all certain about this.)

It was Lydia who settled the matter. "I suggest that Epaphroditus take Onesimus to Rome. I understand that when Paul lived in Ephesus, he met Philemon there and led him to faith in the Savior. Philemon is far more in debt to Paul than Onesimus is to Philemon. Let *Paul* be Onesimus's advocate to Philemon."

The name *Paul* caused everyone to agree with Lydia's suggestion.

"But Paul may tell Philemon to have me killed!" blurted out Onesimus.

There was a spontaneous roar of laughter from everyone. Epaphras ruffled Onesimus's blond hair and reassured him: "The man who himself had others killed and was forgiven? No, Onesimus, he would be the last person on this earth to make such a recommendation."

Lydia joined in: "While Onesimus is here, have someone read to him a copy of Paul's letter to the Galatians. Let Onesimus hear how Paul feels about slavery and freedom."

A few days later the ecclesia in Philippi handed an *enormous* gift to Epaphras to be given to Paul . . . enough of a gift to meet *any* and *all* of Paul's needs. There were letters, too. One was from the church, signed by everyone. The letter expressed to Paul all that Epaphras had done for the Philippians. Epaphras was not at all aware of the letter's contents.

Essentially, the letter said: "Send Epaphras back to us. We request that when he leaves Rome, he come back by way of Philippi and stay among us—and among the other churches in northern Greece—for an extended length of time."

As Epaphras and Onesimus stood beside a ship bound for Rome, there was a time of prayer for Paul. It was prayer so fervent that—like a time of prayer in Jerusalem—it seemed to shake the earth.

Such a great change had come over Onesimus that many cried at his departure as well as at Epaphras's. Some weeks later that ship would dock at Puteoli, from whence the two men would walk to Rome.

What happened next is a tale still told to this day. It is the story of men Paul trained in Ephesus and what they did when they came to Rome. It is a story of Paul and Caesar. But it is also the story of the runaway slave who showed up quite unexpectedly in the Imperial City.

Epaphras was not the only one making his way to Rome. Paul had hardly reached Rome when Titus and Timothy, as well as Tychicus and Trophimus, were on their way. Secundus and Sopater arrived in Rome shortly after the other men did.

Luke and Aristarchus were already there beside Paul. Some time later, John Mark also arrived, having responded to Paul's urgent request. Paul was anxious to hear firsthand the state of the Jewish churches. (As I, Gaius, have said before, I alone was not part of this happy reunion.)

The seven men all arrived within a few days of one another. As soon as they arrived, the men were taken straight to the room where Paul resided. Seeing Paul in chains, they embraced him in a mutual flood of tears. (Always a guard was present. You must know that if any soldier stayed as long as a month in Paul's room, that soldier usually ended up in the household of Christ.)

In the days following, these men also saw Rome, and they were dumbfounded at what they saw.

It seems good to me to tell you what Rome is *really* like because there are many misunderstandings about that city. Each of us, having arrived in Rome, saw our preconceptions die quickly. Although I did not see Rome until several years later, we all agreed it was the closest thing to hell this world contained.

Aristarchus and Luke had warned Timothy and Titus about the terrible conditions of the Imperial City, but warnings are not effective to prepare anyone for them. So it was with Secundus, Sopater, Epaphras, Tychicus, and Trophimus.

My reaction was worse since I came from a very small village. Large cities were something quite foreign to me. (I saw Rome but once and hoped I would never see it again.)

We could not help but marvel that Priscilla and Aquila had been willing to return to this place.

It was Secundus, with his ever-present wit, who one day murmured: "The pit of fire would be an improvement over this place."

The philosopher Seneca made this observation: "If you are going to live in Rome, you would be a blessed man indeed if you were deaf!" Paul had always hoped to come to Rome because it was the capital of most of the world. But, like the rest of us, he had an idea in his head as to what the city would be. It did not even come close to his expectations.

I have always admired Timothy and Titus for what they did once they recovered from their reaction. After reporting to the assembly, which met in Priscilla's house, they entered Rome's marketplaces.

Timothy went to the Jewish markets, Titus to the Latin marketplace, and both went to the Greek marketplaces. How they managed preaching in that stench all day is beyond me. This I can tell you: their bravery inspired Paul's other coworkers to do the same. Not long after, to everyone's surprise, brothers in the assembly made their way into the markets and began proclaiming Christ. (As a result, the church grew in number.)

What is Rome like?

You have heard of the numberless marble buildings. It is

true that almost every important building in the city is covered in beautifully polished marble. The architecture is beyond the imagination of man. The marbled part of the city reaches for several miles. There are statues everywhere. The temples are grand. There are eleven aqueducts that bring water to the city, and all are ornately decorated. They not only convey water but are architectural marvels.

The Circus Maximus, which is 1,800 feet long and 600 feet wide, can hold 150,000 people. It is the largest stadium ever built. I doubt that there will ever again be one so large. Massive walls surround the city. Most were built two and three hundred years ago. Nor are they ordinary walls. They, too, are ornamental masterpieces. The basilicas of the city rise two and three stories high. If you are like me, you would not know what basilicas are. They are buildings built for Rome to carry on business when it is raining! Otherwise, most business is conducted out in the open. The basilicas are built without windows or doors so people can come out of the cold and the rain, yet carry on their business in spacious surroundings. The basilicas have many arches that let in light. They are usually three tiers high with light coming in from all directions.

And the baths! Who could ever even begin to explain the baths? Everyone from the emperor on down, it seems, goes to these buildings every day. Each person goes through a long involved process of bathing. It is said that one of the former emperors came to the baths seven times a day. It is a wonder he ever had time to rule the empire!

Then there are the seven hills of Rome. The first ever inhabited was the Palatine. It slopes down to a vast pasture and then rises again to another hill—Aventine. This is where Priscilla's home was located before it burned down in the great fire.

There are the vestal virgins, picked out around the age of seven and then prepared for carrying on the rituals of the goddess Vesta. These women are released from their duties at the age of thirty-seven. Because their bodies must never be touched nor their bones broken, if a vestal virgin ever breaks her vow, she is buried alive.

There are vast warehouses filled with grain, supplying everyone's needs. An artificial island has been built in the Tiber River that serves as a harbor for the ships that navigate the river all the way to Rome. There are villas everywhere. The walls of the rooms are covered with vast mosaics and paintings. I understand Augustus built a magnificent palace, but Nero had it torn down to build his Golden House, which with its gardens, took up nearly one-third of the city's space. (Later the emperor Vespasian tore down this palace to rid the nation, and the world, of the memories of Nero and his atrocities.)

It is this marvelous city, with its Senate, marching soldiers, triumphant parades, arches of triumph, baths, pillars, and temples—such as the Pantheon—that all men and women see in their imaginations as being *Rome*.

True, all of this can be found in Rome. But that is only half the story. It is less than half the story!

What we never hear about is the noise and the stench.

No animals, grain, or even carts are allowed into the city during the daytime. But all through the day, endless wagons and a sea of animals gather outside the walls and wait for the night. When night comes, the people get off the streets. Then the city is deluged by cows, geese, ducks, sheep, goats, and pigs pouring into every nook and crevice of the city. Their owners and keepers are soon screaming at the top of their lungs. There is *never* a night this is not going on. And when the night is over, the streets are filthy beyond human description. (If you venture out at night, the chances are good that you will either be run over by the cattle or knocked in the head by waiting thieves. In all the streets and alleys, there are those waiting to rob you.)

Seneca said that while in Rome he literally lived on the rooftop. He did so to get away from the stench and the noise.

Should you walk the streets during the day, you will see virtually everybody with a flower or a scented cloth against their nose, trying to cancel out the unbelievable smell of this filthy place.

Wide streets are generally about fifteen feet wide, with five feet on each side for walking. The middle five feet is the city's sewerage. The middle is deeper than the sidewalks, and there all the filth of man and animals lies until the sewage piles up higher than the sidewalks. You can collapse just from breathing the stench. Once the sewage is higher than the sidewalks, every person in Rome prays for a torrential rain that will wash this horrendous garbage out of the city and into the stinking Tiber River. If rains are torrential, there will be a few days when the city loses its staggering odor.

For those who can own a home, there are two kinds. One is the home that is boxed in on all sides. In the center of the house is an atrium. All rooms lead toward the middle of the house, where an open roof lets water fall into an awaiting pond. It is here, in this room, that the family spends most of its time, because the noise is slightly muffled. If all the windows and doors are closed, sometimes the stench is bearable.

The other kind of home, if a man could call it that, is the insula—an apartment. Most people do not own these apartments but only rent them.

A building can contain an almost endless number of apartments. The buildings are usually five stories high. The first story is always rented out as shops to those who have something to sell. All day long men yell out to passersby, telling them of the superiority of their goods.

The second to the fifth floors are actually made up of small rooms, usually about eight feet by ten feet, or ten feet by twelve feet. Unlike the homes with an atrium, these apartments are not built toward the interior but the exterior. The home looks out upon the street below. The noise comes in without restriction. So also does the smell. Nor is that all. Without even looking down, those in the apartment are constantly throwing their garbage, water, human waste, and even broken pots onto the streets below. To walk the narrow streets of Rome is, quite literally, to risk your life.

In the summer, people in the insulae sleep on the rooftops. You might discover every human being on the roof during the hot days of July and August. As a result, the roofs often cave in. Almost every day you hear of the collapse of an insula with most of the people involved being injured or even killed. Nonetheless, this is where most people live during the summertime in Rome.

And in the winter? Those who have homes or insulae—and they are not the majority—may not freeze. Nonetheless, every day during winter, bodies are hauled out of the city, having died of cold and exposure the night before.

With all of that, I have not yet mentioned the worst: the living conditions of the slaves.

A little over half of all the people in Rome are slaves. (As I pen these words, there are about one million people living in the city of Rome.) This means about five hundred thousand slaves live in Rome. All those vast, beautiful temples are built by slaves and freed slaves. So also is every beautiful building in Rome. All day long, from the beginning of earliest light until night, the bricks are made and the bricks are laid. The marble is hewn and polished and polished some more. The entire city, as magnificent as it is, has been built and maintained by men and women who were captured in other countries and shipped to the Imperial City. They are set to work building the magnificence that is Rome.

Where do the slaves sleep? They sleep on the streets—or at least they try to sleep. There can be no true sleep at night. Many people in Rome die simply from lack of rest. The poor, the freed slaves, and the slaves sleep in doorways, on the pedestals of statues—anywhere that it is safe from the cattle.

Some people sleep on the ground outside the city, but the weather is no kinder there than within the city.

The average life of a slave? Most never see the age of thirty. The average age of a woman here, or in any part of the empire, is around twenty-nine. People are considered old when they are forty. (Paul of Tarsus amazingly—considering all the suffering he passed through—lived to be about sixty.)

The life of slaves who work in villas is only sightly better— they sleep on the floor in the halls. And in the palaces there are vast stairwells leading deep into the ground with slots built into the earth along the way, each just big enough for a person to lie down in. Some of these underground labyrinths have places for a hundred or more slaves. There is no air down there.

Only a few of the people who live in Rome enjoy its beauty. The majority daily labor to bring ease and pleasure to these few.

Each day a slave receives what is essentially the amount of grain two hands can hold. This is his total pay throughout his entire life. With few exceptions, a slave has but the garment that is on his back. It will be the only one he will own as long as he lives. It will be patched, but it will never be replaced.

Such is Rome.

This is why there are the games. This is why the Circus Maximus exists. This is why there are the baths. The only slight pleasures the extremely poor have are the games and the baths.

I, Gaius, have attempted to give you some idea of what Rome is really like. The political intrigue is beyond the grasp of most of us. What goes on in Caesar's household is nothing but endless intrigue. The Senate, on the other hand, is but a symbol of the past republic. The truth is, Caesar is all the government there is.

What I have just told you is what we all saw when we arrived in Rome, which caused Paul's coworkers to gasp at what their eyes and noses told them. With that said, we must turn to those incredible events that took place in the city during Paul's imprisonment.

We will begin with Epaphras and that terrified runaway slave, Onesimus.

CHAPTER 8

Like the others, when Epaphras arrived in Rome, he had been taken straight to Paul's rented room. Paul's joy soon turned to dismay as he heard Epaphras tell the story of Onesimus.

When Onesimus was brought to Paul, the apostle to the Gentiles addressed him in clear and certain words: "You knew you were asking for your own death when you chose to leave Philemon and follow Epaphras, did you not?"

Onesimus nodded and began to cry.

Paul said, "Whether you live or whether you die, there is something you must do. You must pray for salvation from Christ."

"I want to. I want to."

"Completely? Utterly? Absolutely? With Christ always in first place?"

"What else is there in this world for me?"

Epaphras broke in. "Philemon said that you always failed to bow to him. Is that true?"

Onesimus turned crimson. "Yes, it's true," he said sheepishly.

"Will you now kneel to Christ, the risen Savior?"

"Yes. Yes, to him I will kneel—gladly, gladly."

Paul placed his hand on Onesimus's head and said, "Ask

him for the salvation of your soul and spirit. Then we shall all pray for the salvation of your body."

Onesimus knelt and, like a little child, began to speak to Christ, pouring out his heart in gentle sobs. He asked forgiveness for his stubbornness and self-will, placing all his hope and his future in the risen Lord.

Epaphras reached down and pulled Onesimus into his arms. "His Master has forgiven him everything!"

Onesimus buried his face in Epaphras's chest and cried the more. Finally he looked up. "Forgiven?"

"Yes, by the Master of your master. And now, at last, Onesimus you are free . . . inside. You are a believer now. You should not run. If Philemon is not willing to let you live . . . you are a Christian . . . you can die."

Onesimus breathed deeply, a slight smile just barely visible. "Yes, Christ is mine. I can die."

Paul rejoiced at the salvation of this lost sheep.

After this moving exchange with Epaphras and Onesimus, Paul sent them out of the room and asked Epaphras to summon the Eight, the men who had sat at Paul's feet in Ephesus. These followers had reassembled in Rome and were once more learning from their mentor, who now spoke to them in chains. Paul spoke as though he would be beheaded by Nero, and the men listened as though this would be true. He implored them to *always* look to one another and depend on one another. Nonetheless, as he talked, he made each man responsible for some specific area of the Roman Empire.

Paul asked question upon question about every assembly. And there were questions he had never asked before, for he inquired about the political situation in each province. He was especially concerned about the growing unrest in Jerusalem and other parts of the world.

Paul was emphatic about having one of the Eight on the island of Malta. Every man in the room, having heard Luke and

Aristarchus recount the incredible story of what happened on Malta, was eager to volunteer.

Titus had been the first to depart Rome. He returned to Antioch with news of Paul and then went on to visit Crete.

For several mornings the assembly in Rome gathered to hear Epaphras's report, as well as Onesimus's story—and to hear from their sister church in Philippi.

And for a few days thereafter, Epaphras and Onesimus, being from a rural setting, wandered agog through the streets of the Imperial City.

"I never saw so many people," said Onesimus. "No wonder the armies of Rome defeated my people. We had no chance. My father should have fled, not fought. We would be safe today beyond the Danube. And look at all the people with painted hands. Half of Rome's people are slaves."

Epaphroditus's thoughts were elsewhere. *How can we ever reach these people? There are too many of them*, he thought.

A few days later Epaphroditus made the following declaration to the church. "I am so grateful for your hospitality, but I feel I must live with Paul."

Onesimus followed, "I am a slave. I am now at peace with this. I failed Philemon. But here I can be what is God's will for me. I wish also to be with Paul—a slave to a slave of Christ."

Onesimus's eyes filled with tears. "If I had not been captured on the frontiers I would never have come to know my Lord who now lives in me. Now, I . . . a slave . . . desire to be *his* slave. I can do no better than to live at the feet of a man whose very life is Christ!"

"How can you know these things? You are a new Christian," someone asked with deep emotion.

"I . . . I . . . do not know how I know. But when one of the brothers read the Galatian letter to me . . . "

Everyone broke out in applause.

The next day Epaphroditus and Onesimus moved—Onesimus, making his bed at the feet of Paul, Epaphroditus in a room next door to Paul's.

It was during this time that Epaphroditus gave Paul the letter and the gift from Philippi. "I have many letters with me from the holy ones in Philippi to the holy ones in Rome." With that Epaphroditus unceremoniously handed the gift to Paul. "It is from the entire church in Philippi."

"So," said Paul, "Philippi, my beloved Philippi! Their generosity has exceeded that of all the other churches combined. They understand the Lord's work. They understand the worker's needs—that he has need of money for the work, not for himself. It appears that most of the other assemblies feel that an archangel comes down and provides for the necessities of life *and* for the expenses of the work!"

(You can be assured that the gift from Philippi was one that would pay Paul's expenses for his entire two-year stay in Rome.)

Paul motioned to Epaphroditus to sit down. "A runaway slave. Philemon must be angry. Three new churches in eastern Asia Minor. A month in Philippi. As you see, I have much time, please tell me the entire story."

And quite a story it was that Epaphras told.

CHAPTER 9

Now, at your request," said Paul, "I am to write a letter to the assembly in Colosse.

"I understand you are called Epaphroditus when you are in Greece? Although you have only asked me to write *one* letter to Colosse, may I write *two* letters instead? Both will be written to circulate in eastern Asia Minor. Both letters will go not only to Colosse but also to Hierapolis and Laodicea.

"I want to write the first letter on the subject of Christ— Christ as he is *now* in other realms, *and* Christ as he was before creation—the eternal Christ, the Son of God."

Epaphroditus's eyes sparkled. "Of course. That would be far more than I expected."

"Good," replied Paul. "That will be the context of the first letter. As to the second, I desire to write to your brothers and sisters in Colosse."

Epaphroditus choked. "Oh, Paul, I beseech you to do so."

"So be it. First a letter concerning the Christ. Then a letter concerning the church."

"Now, I need several days . . . alone if at all possible. Of course, I need an amanuensis [scribe]. Poor Timothy, he hates that role. Nonetheless, it will probably be Timothy who helps me in this undertaking."

It is my honor to tell you of these two letters, which are, in my judgment, Paul's master prose, never to be surpassed by anyone, even until the day the Lord returns.

As Paul began to write the letter to the church in Colosse, he was constantly shuffling his chains in an effort to find a place where the fetters did not cut his wrists.

The letter would be only five pages long, yet each time I read it, I feel that it was written not by the hand of a man, but by a heavenly messenger!

As the years rolled by, copies of this letter found their way into every ecclesia in Asia Minor. Colossians *is* the most Christ-centered book this world will ever know.

For those of you who have never read this incredible letter to Colosse, I, Gaius, feel conpelled to urge you to read it. It is centered so much in the other realm. Only a devout old man who had lived his entire life in the Lord's presence—a man so broken, a man who had visited that unseen realm—could ever pen such a piece of literature.

These are my own feelings, but they were shared by all of us when we read this letter. The person who felt strongest about the magnificence of this letter was the man who sat beside Paul as the letter came into being. Timothy often spoke of that hour, and it was from him that I learned the details of that day.

This letter is from Paul, chosen by God to be an apostle of Christ Jesus, and from our brother Timothy.

It is written to God's holy people in the city of Colosse, who are faithful brothers and sisters in Christ.

May God our Father give you grace and peace.

The Colossians were stunned to receive a letter from Paul and equally amazed to see that Paul had sent Tychicus all the way from Rome to deliver the letter.

Before the day was over, the Colossians had made two cop-

ies of this letter, one copy to Laodicea and one to Hierapolis.
When the letter was read to the assembly, the following words
filled them with wonder:

> We always pray for you, and we give thanks to God
> the Father of our Lord Jesus Christ, for we have heard
> that you trust in Christ Jesus and that you love all of
> God's people. You do this because you are looking
> forward to the joys of heaven—as you have been ever
> since you first heard the truth of the Good News. This
> same Good News that came to you is going out all
> over the world. It is changing lives everywhere, just
> as it changed yours that very first day you heard and
> understood the truth about God's great kindness to
> sinners.

Someone in the assembly, listening to this part, said,
"Thank God that the Lord saved Epaphras in Ephesus and sent
him back to us. It was as though that brother had anticipated
Paul's words."

> Epaphras, our much loved co-worker, was the one
> who brought you the Good News. He is Christ's faith-
> ful servant, and he is helping us in your place. He is the
> one who told us about the great love for others that
> the Holy Spirit has given you. So we have continued
> praying for you ever since we first heard about you.
> We ask God to give you a complete understanding
> of what he wants to do in your lives, and we ask him to
> make you wise with spiritual wisdom. Then the way
> you live will always honor and please the Lord, and
> you will continually do good, kind things for others.
> All the while, you will learn to know God better and
> better.

By this point there were many in the room crying quietly.

We also pray that you will be strengthened with his glorious power so that you will have all the patience and endurance you need. May you be filled with joy, always thanking the Father, who has enabled you to share the inheritance that belongs to God's holy people, who live in the light. For he has rescued us from the one who rules in the kingdom of darkness, and he has brought us into the Kingdom of his dear Son. God has purchased our freedom with his blood and has forgiven all our sins.

Quiet prayer began to emerge all across the room as those beautiful words flowed on. One sister even said, "I never knew that those of us here in Colosse were so wonderful."

Paul's next words rose into the other realm, revealing things which none of us had ever known before. The man who had been taken up to the third heaven was, at last, beginning to reveal to us a little of what he had seen and heard.

Christ is the visible image of the invisible God. He existed before God made anything at all and is supreme over all creation. Christ is the one through whom God created everything in heaven and earth. He made the things we can see and the things we can't see—kings, kingdoms, rulers, and authorities. Everything has been created through him and for him. He existed before everything else began, and he holds all creation together.

Throughout most of his life, Paul was committed to but two things, Christ and his church. That was never made clearer than when Paul told us of Christ's view of the church:

Christ is the head of the church, which is his body.

Then Paul continued showing us the supreme place *Christ* took as seen through the eyes of God:

> He is the first of all who will rise from the dead, so he is first in everything. For God in all his fullness was pleased to live in Christ, and by him God reconciled everything to himself. He made peace with everything in heaven and on earth by means of his blood on the cross. This includes you who were once so far away from God.

By now virtually every saint in Colosse was crying. And why not? Paul had written these words so intimately and beautifully, it was as though Christ had died specifically for the believers in Colosse.

> You were his enemies, separated from him by your evil thoughts and actions, yet now he has brought you back as his friends. He has done this through his death on the cross in his own human body. As a result, he has brought you into the very presence of God, and you are holy and blameless as you stand before him without a single fault. But you must continue to believe this truth and stand in it firmly. Don't drift away from the assurance you received when you heard the Good News. The Good News has been preached all over the world, and I, Paul, have been appointed by God to proclaim it.

At this point Paul's words became even more personal. He wrote (and believed) that he was suffering in Rome for the assembly in Colosse.

> I am glad when I suffer for you [Colossians] in my body, for I am completing what remains of Christ's sufferings

for his body, the church. God has given me the responsibility of serving his church by proclaiming his message in all its fullness to you Gentiles.

What followed was something none of us had ever heard Paul make so clear: God's hidden mystery—hidden from even the prophets—was that God was going to reveal his Son to the Gentiles. Even more, God himself has entered into each believing Gentile by his Spirit and thereby made himself *one* with Gentiles.

This message was kept secret for centuries and generations past, but now it has been revealed to his own holy people. For it has pleased God to tell his people that the riches and glory of Christ are for you Gentiles, too. For this is the secret: Christ lives in you, and this is your assurance that you will share in his glory.

So everywhere we go, we tell everyone about Christ. We warn them and teach them with all the wisdom God has given us, for we want to present them to God, perfect in their relationship to Christ. I work very hard at this, as I depend on Christ's mighty power that works within me.

Now came the heartbreaker. Paul's next words brought sobs and quiet praise, not only to the believers in Colosse, but also in Laodicea and Hierapolis.

I want you to know how much I have agonized for you and for the church at Laodicea, and for many other friends who have never known me personally. My goal is that they will be encouraged and knit together by strong ties of love. I want them to have full confidence because they have complete understanding of God's se-

cret plan, which is Christ himself. In him lie hidden all
the treasures of wisdom and knowledge.

"Christ, Christ, Christ," the Colossians began to whisper.
The man who was reading the letter to the Colossian church
stopped as one believer after another began to lift up prayer and
praise to Christ. The reader then continued:

> I am telling you this so that no one will be able to de-
> ceive you with persuasive arguments. For though I am
> far away from you, my heart is with you. And I am very
> happy because you are living as you should and because
> of your strong faith in Christ.
>
> And now, just as you accepted Christ Jesus as your
> Lord, you must continue to live in obedience to him.
> Let your roots grow down into him and draw up nour-
> ishment from him, so you will grow in faith, strong and
> vigorous in the truth you were taught. Let your lives
> overflow with thanksgiving for all he has done.
>
> Don't let anyone lead you astray with empty phi-
> losophy and high-sounding nonsense that come from
> human thinking and from the evil powers of this world,
> and not from Christ. For in Christ the fullness of God
> lives in a human body, and you are complete through
> your union with Christ. He is the Lord over every ruler
> and authority in the universe.

Had Paul been able to watch the Colossian believers' reaction to his words, he would have known *no one* was going to
draw this people away from Christ.

> When you came to Christ, you were "circumcised," but
> not by a physical procedure. It was a spiritual proce-
> dure—the cutting away of your sinful nature. For you

were buried with Christ when you were baptized. And with him you were raised to a new life because you trusted the mighty power of God, who raised Christ from the dead.

By this point in Paul's life and in the life of the churches, anytime Paul said "circumcised" they knew he was warning them about legalistic Jews who visited Paul's churches and tried to circumcise the Gentile men according to the harshness of Jewish law.

You were dead because of your sins and because your sinful nature was not yet cut away. Then God made you alive with Christ. He forgave all our sins. He canceled the record that contained the charges against us. He took it and destroyed it by nailing it to Christ's cross. In this way, God disarmed the evil rulers and authorities. He shamed them publicly by his victory over them on the cross of Christ.

Paul's next words could not have been clearer. Christ had done away with the commands and ordinances of Judaism.

So don't let anyone condemn you for what you eat or drink, or for not celebrating certain holy days or new-moon ceremonies or Sabbaths. For these rules were only shadows of the real thing, Christ himself. Don't let anyone condemn you by insisting on self-denial. And don't let anyone say you must worship angels, even though they say they have had visions about this. These people claim to be so humble, but their sinful minds have made them proud. But they are not connected to Christ, the head of the body. For we are joined together in his body by his strong sinews, and we grow only as we get our nourishment and strength from God.

At this point, someone in the room cried out, "Free from the law!" Another cried, "Free from all Pharisees except one ex-Pharisee!"

You have died with Christ, and he has set you free from the evil powers of this world. So why do you keep on following rules of the world, such as, "Don't handle, don't eat, don't touch." Such rules are mere human teaching about things that are gone as soon as we use them. These rules may seem wise because they require strong devotion, humility, and severe bodily discipline. But they have no effect when it comes to conquering a person's evil thoughts and desires.

At these stirring words, brothers and sisters began to stand and call out, "No more do's! No more don'ts!" At that moment one brother cried out, "We must write Paul and tell him, 'We are free from all these rules. We died to them, in Christ.'"

Since you have been raised to new life with Christ, set your sights on the realities of heaven, where Christ sits at God's right hand in the place of honor and power. Let heaven fill your thoughts. Do not think only about things down here on earth. For you died when Christ died, and your real life is hidden with Christ in God. And when Christ, who is your real life, is revealed to the whole world, you will share in all his glory.

The reader stopped. The room had broken out in pandemonium as brothers and sisters began to exhort one another and declare their freedom in Christ—to God!

So put to death the sinful, earthly things lurking within you. Have nothing to do with sexual sin, impurity, lust, and shameful desires. Don't be greedy for the good things of this life, for that is idolatry. God's terrible anger will come upon those who do such things. You used to do them when your life was still part of this world. But now is the time to get rid of anger, rage, malicious behavior, slander, and dirty language. Don't lie to each other, for you have stripped off your old evil nature and all its wicked deeds. In its place you have clothed yourselves with a brand-new nature that is continually being renewed as you learn more and more about Christ, who created this new nature within you. In this new life, it doesn't matter if you are a Jew or a Gentile, circumcised or uncircumcised, barbaric, uncivilized, slave, or free. Christ is all that matters, and he lives in all of us.

Since God chose you to be the holy people whom he loves, you must clothe yourselves with tenderhearted mercy, kindness, humility, gentleness, and patience. You must make allowance for each other's faults and forgive the person who offends you. Remember, the Lord forgave you, so you must forgive others. And the most important piece of clothing you must wear is love. Love is what binds us all together in perfect harmony. And let the peace that comes from Christ rule in your hearts. For as members of one body you are all called to live in peace. And always be thankful.

Let the words of Christ, in all their richness, live in your hearts and make you wise. Use his words to teach and counsel each other. Sing psalms and hymns and spiritual songs to God with thankful hearts. And whatever you do or say, let it be as a representative of the Lord Jesus, all the while giving thanks through him to God the Father.

The reader stopped again. This time he spoke, "Let us all get close to one another and speak to the Lord about all these things."

A moment later everyone stood and began pressing in closer to one another. The praise, encouragement, and exhaltation that followed continued for over an hour.

It was late, but *no one* was about to go home! The reading therefore continued with Paul's practical advice.

You wives must submit to your husbands, as is fitting for those who belong to the Lord. And you husbands must love your wives and never treat them harshly.

You children must always obey your parents, for this is what pleases the Lord. Fathers, don't aggravate your children. If you do, they will become discouraged and quit trying.

After advice to families, Paul addressed slaves and their masters. There was a hush in the assembly as many were sobered by this practical and spiritual advice.

You slaves must obey your earthly masters in everything you do. Try to please them all the time, not just when they are watching you. Obey them willingly because of your reverent fear of the Lord. Work hard and cheerfully at whatever you do, as though you were working for the Lord rather than for people. Remember that the Lord will give you an inheritance as your reward, and the Master you are serving is Christ. But if you do what is wrong, you will be paid back for the wrong you have done. For God has no favorites who can get away with evil.

You slave owners must be just and fair to your slaves. Remember that you also have a Master—in heaven.

Devote yourselves to prayer with an alert mind and a thankful heart. Don't forget to pray for us, too, that God will give us many opportunities to preach about his secret plan—that Christ is also for you Gentiles. That is why I am here in chains. Pray that I will proclaim this message as clearly as I should.

Live wisely among those who are not Christians, and make the most of every opportunity. Let your conversation be gracious and effective so that you will have the right answer for everyone.

Paul's final words were about Tychicus coming to report on the situation in Rome. Notice that Paul gives Onesimus equal standing with Tychicus, despite the fact he is a runaway slave under sentence of death. This was just one example of how Paul meant to ensure Onesimus's safety.

Paul then added greetings from Mark, Justus, and Aristarchus.

Paul's words about Epaphras were, as always, the highest words of commendation Paul ever made about anyone!

Tychicus, a much loved brother, will tell you how I am getting along. He is a faithful helper who serves the Lord with me. I have sent him on this special trip to let you know how we are doing and to encourage you. I am also sending Onesimus, a faithful and much loved brother, one of your own people. He and Tychicus will give you all the latest news.

Aristarchus, who is in prison with me, sends you his greetings, and so does Mark, Barnabas's cousin. And as you were instructed before, make Mark welcome if he comes your way. Jesus (the one we call Justus) also sends his greetings. These are the only Jewish Christians among my co-workers; they are working with me here for the Kingdom of God. And what a comfort they have been!

Epaphras, from your city, a servant of Christ Jesus, sends you his greetings. He always prays earnestly for you, asking God to make you strong and perfect, fully confident of the whole will of God. I can assure you that he has agonized for you and also for the Christians in Laodicea and Hierapolis.

Dear Doctor Luke sends his greetings, and so does Demas. Please give my greetings to our Christian brothers and sisters at Laodicea, and to Nympha and those who meet in her house.

After you have read this letter, pass it on to the church at Laodicea so they can read it, too. And you should read the letter I wrote to them.

The Laodiceans were all smiles when they heard that Paul had not forgotten them and even knew in whose house they met!

And say to Archippus, "Be sure to carry out the work the Lord gave you."

Here is my greeting in my own handwriting— PAUL.

Remember my chains.

May the grace of God be with you.

Shortly after Paul finished the letter to Colosse, he let it be known that he wished a day of solitude to consider a second circuit letter, one concerning the bride of Christ. Like the first letter, it was intended for the assemblies in Laodicea, Colosse, and Hierapolis. Once this letter was sent out, it seemed every gathering in Asia Minor wanted a copy, including the Ephesian church.

Is it possible to explain that second letter? I doubt it! As for me, I believe Paul's decision to pen an epistle concerning the ecclesia of Christ will probably go on affecting the lives of believers until Jesus comes.

Here is the story of that incomparable masterpiece of literature.

CHAPTER 10

Paul said, "Epaphras, sit here with me while Timothy and I pen another letter to the churches in eastern Asia Minor. I wrote of Christ in the first letter. I will now write about Christ's body, about the ecclesia, the bride of Christ.

"If Caesar sees fit to remove my head from my body, then I will say unequivocally that these will not only be my last two letters but the *highest* I have ever written. One letter exalts my Lord, the Lord of the cosmos—the other exalts his bride, the church. The Man who is the head, and the woman who is his body."

That letter was truly unique in that Paul wrote to the ecclesia about the ecclesia. He covered so much in so few pages that even until this day the letter staggers my mind. I have read it more often than any other letter Paul wrote.

(Before you read this wonderful letter, please keep in mind that both letters were written to churches, not to individuals.)

Paul began the letter by decreeing that the riches of the other realm belong to all the holy ones who gather together. Paul meant that statement. Like the individual, to some degree a church, corporately, also has a spirit; and because that spirit has come forth from other realms we, as an assembly, can dare visit that realm in spirit. While we are still upon the earth, we can touch the other realm.

I hereby present to you the letter which was addressed to Colosse, Hierapolis, and Laodicea, but which took wings and soon circulated throughout the empire. Observe how Paul blends into one the most exalted thoughts this earth can ever know—the oneness of the body of Christ with her Lord.

> This letter is from Paul, chosen by God to be an apostle of Christ Jesus.
> It is written . . .

Paul paused. "Timothy, even though this letter is going to Colosse, Laodicea, and Hierapolis, most of the churches in Asia Minor, including Ephesus, will probably make copies. It would therefore be wise to leave a blank here, at least for this final copy. We will fill in the blank space with the name of each assembly when other copies are made."

Paul continued his letter:

> . . . to God's holy people in Ephesus, who are faithful followers of Christ Jesus.
> May grace and peace be yours, sent to you from God our Father and Jesus Christ our Lord.
> How we praise God, the Father of our Lord Jesus Christ, who has blessed us with every spiritual blessing in the heavenly realms because we belong to Christ.

Paul stopped speaking. "All believers need to know they were existing inside Christ *before* he created the world."

> Long ago, even before he made the world, God loved us and chose us in Christ to be holy and without fault in his eyes.

"Ah! In *his* eyes we are holy and perfect. Not so in our eyes. We need to see ourselves through God's eyes!"

His unchanging plan has always been to adopt us into his own family by bringing us to himself through Jesus Christ. And this gave him great pleasure.

So we praise God for the wonderful kindness he has poured out on us because we belong to his dearly loved Son. He is so rich in kindness that he purchased our freedom through the blood of his Son, and our sins are forgiven. He has showered his kindness on us, along with all wisdom and understanding.

"Would that every believer could begin life in Christ knowing this."

God's secret plan has now been revealed to us; it is a plan centered on Christ, designed long ago according to his good pleasure. And this is his plan: At the right time he will bring everything together under the authority of Christ—everything in heaven and on earth.

"*That* is God's mystery. His great, hidden secret. On earth a carpenter in Galilee . . . before creation he was Lord. *Now* preeminent in *all* things."

Furthermore, because of Christ, we have received an inheritance from God, for he chose us from the beginning, and all things happen just as he decided long ago. God's purpose was that we [Jews] who were the first to trust in Christ should praise our glorious God. And now you [Gentiles] also have heard the truth, the Good News that God saves you. And when you believed in Christ, he identified you as his own . . .

"Yes!" exclaimed Paul, utterly caught up in the thought of the endless riches of Christ. "He made heathen Gentiles his very own—and gave them an indwelling Holy Spirit. Write that!"

... by giving you the Holy Spirit, whom he promised long ago. The Spirit is God's guarantee that he will give us everything he promised and that he has purchased us to be his own people. This is just one more reason for us to praise our glorious God.

"Now, Epaphras, I must tell them the joy I had when I heard that you raised up *three* assemblies in those three cities in eastern Asia Minor. It was a total surprise to me because I was so centered on seeing churches raised up in the cities near Ephesus."

Ever since I first heard of your strong faith in the Lord Jesus and your love for Christians everywhere, I have never stopped thanking God for you. I pray for you constantly, asking God, the glorious Father of our Lord Jesus Christ, to give you spiritual wisdom and understanding, so that you might grow in your knowledge of God.

"Revelation! My prayer is that they have revelation!"

I pray that your hearts will be flooded with light so that you can understand the wonderful future he has promised to those he called. I want you to realize what a rich and glorious inheritance he has given to his people.

I pray that you will begin to understand the incredible greatness of his power for us who believe him. This is the same mighty power that raised Christ from the dead and seated him in the place of honor at God's right hand in the heavenly realms.

"Power, yes, power to finish his work in us . . . and to *keep* us during the process.

"Let me see, have I told them of the Lord, as he is one state—that he is Lord over all? No! I have not. I will now!"

Now he is far above any ruler or authority or power or leader or anything else in this world or in the world to come. And God has put all things under the authority of Christ, and he gave him this authority for the benefit of the church.

"Yes!" Paul exclaimed again. "They must know the centrality of the church . . . even the church of which they are part!"

And the church is his body; it is filled by Christ, who fills everything everywhere with his presence.

Once you were dead, doomed forever because of your many sins. You used to live just like the rest of the world, full of sin, obeying Satan, the mighty prince of the power of the air. He is the spirit at work in the hearts of those who refuse to obey God. All of us used to live that way, following the passions and desires of our evil nature. We were born with an evil nature, and we were under God's anger just like everyone else.

Paul began to weep. "A dark picture I have just painted! But . . . God! But God!"

But God is so rich in mercy, and he loved us so very much, that even while we were dead because of our sins, he gave us life when he raised Christ from the dead.

(It is only by God's special favor that you have been saved!) For he raised us from the dead along with Christ . . .

Paul began to weep again, and with a wondering voice said to Timothy and Epaphras, "I rose from the dead when Christ was raised from the dead. In past eternity I was *in* him. When he arose, I was *still* in him!"

. . . and we are seated with him in the heavenly realms—all because we are one with Christ Jesus.

"Timothy! Is it clear? That we are utterly *one* with Christ. Have I made that clear to them? Seated in Christ—in the other realm. That is where we really are!"

Timothy could not answer for he, too, was weeping.

And so God can always point to us as examples of the incredible wealth of his favor and kindness toward us, as shown in all he has done for us through Christ Jesus.

God saved you by his special favor when you believed. And you can't take credit for this; it is a gift from God.

"I *must* emphasize this. Otherwise we will see Gentiles acting like unbelieving Jews who mistakenly think they can save themselves by being good and living a good life. The good comes *after* the unearned, unmerited gift of the mercy and grace of God."

Salvation is not a reward for the good things we have done, so none of us can boast about it. For we are God's masterpiece. He has created us anew in Christ

Jesus, so that we can do the good things he planned for us long ago.

"I suppose I have to say something about circumcision," sighed Paul, "just in case some Jews visit them and while there try to persuade the Gentiles that they have to be circumcised in order to be saved."

Don't forget that you Gentiles used to be outsiders by birth. You were called "the uncircumcised ones" by the Jews, who were proud of their circumcision, even though it affected only their bodies and not their hearts. In those days you were living apart from Christ. You were excluded from God's people, Israel, and you did not know the promises God had made to them. You lived in this world without God and without hope. But now you belong to Christ Jesus. Though you once were far away from God, now you have been brought near to him because of the blood of Christ.

For Christ himself has made peace between us Jews and you Gentiles by making us all one people. He has broken down the wall of hostility that used to separate us.

"Am I going to enjoy this next sentence, Timothy!" Paul then thundered:

By his death he ended the whole system of Jewish law that excluded the Gentiles. His purpose was to make peace between Jews and Gentiles by creating in himself one new person from the two groups. Together as one body, Christ reconciled both groups to God by means of his death, and our hostility toward each other was put to death. He has brought this Good News of peace to you Gentiles who were far away from him, and to us Jews who were near. Now all of us, both Jews and Gentiles, may come to the Father through the same Holy Spirit because of what Christ has done for us.

"Let the party of the circumcised deal with that!"

So now you Gentiles are no longer strangers and foreigners. You are citizens along with all of God's holy people. You are members of God's family. We are his house, built on the foundation of the apostles and the prophets. And the cornerstone is Christ Jesus himself. We who believe are carefully joined together, becoming a holy temple for the Lord. Through him you Gentiles are also joined together as part of this dwelling where God lives by his Spirit.

"Most of those in the three churches in Asia Minor are Gentiles, are they not, Epaphras?"
Epaphras nodded.
"And do they know that I was called to them, to Gentiles, to declare Christ to them?"
Epaphras smiled. "They do. But tell them anyway!"
Paul smiled and took a deep breath.

I, Paul, am a prisoner of Christ Jesus because of my preaching to you Gentiles. As you already know, God has given me this special ministry of announcing his favor to you Gentiles. As I briefly mentioned earlier in this letter, God himself revealed his secret plan to me. As you read what I have written, you will understand what I know about this plan regarding Christ. God did not reveal it to previous generations, but now he has revealed it by the Holy Spirit to his holy apostles and prophets.

"Oh!" said Paul. "I must return to God's mystery! Gentiles must know what God kept as a secret plan, even since the beginning of creation."

And this is the secret plan: The Gentiles have an equal share with the Jews in all the riches inherited by God's children. Both groups have believed the Good News, and both are part of the same body and enjoy together the promise of blessings through Christ Jesus. By God's special favor and mighty power, I have been given the wonderful privilege of serving him by spreading this Good News.

Just think! Though I did nothing to deserve it, and though I am the least deserving Christian there is, I was chosen for this special joy of telling the Gentiles about the endless treasures available to them in Christ. I was chosen to explain to everyone this plan that God, the Creator of all things, had kept secret from the beginning.

God's purpose was to show his wisdom in all its rich variety to all the rulers and authorities in the heavenly realms. They will see this when Jews and Gentiles are joined together in his church. This was his plan from all eternity, and it has now been carried out through Christ Jesus our Lord.

Epaphras, every inch a Gentile, interrupted with a resounding "Praise God!"

Because of Christ and our faith in him, we can now come fearlessly into God's presence, assured of his glad welcome. So please don't despair because of what they are doing to me here. It is for you that I am suffering, so you should feel honored and encouraged.

Yet again Paul fell silent. For a long time he said nothing. Finally he whispered,

> When I think of the wisdom and scope of God's plan, I fall to my knees and pray to the Father, the Creator of everything in heaven and on earth. I pray that from his glorious, unlimited resources he will give you mighty inner strength through his Holy Spirit. And I pray that Christ will be more and more at home in your hearts as you trust in him.

As Paul continued to speak, he wept. "I must exhort them. Christ, oh Christ! They must go deep in Christ. This is the only hope of *any* church!"

> May your roots go down deep into the soil of God's marvelous love. And may you have the power to understand, as all God's people should, how wide, how long, how high, and how deep his love really is. May you experience the love of Christ, though it is so great you will never fully understand it. Then you will be filled . . .

Paul looked up, and turning to Timothy with questioning eyes, he said, "Will they understand that when I say *you*, I am speaking of the entire church—the corporate, functioning body of Christ? We will never be what we ought to be except in the community of believers. In the church even the weakest of all has an excellent chance!"

Paul continued, "That you *all* be filled,"

> . . . with the fullness of life and power that comes from God.
>
> Now glory be to God! By his mighty power at work within us, he is able to accomplish infinitely more than

we would ever dare to ask or hope. May he be given
glory in the church and in Christ Jesus forever and ever
through endless ages. Amen.

Timothy and Epaphras both thought because of this beautiful benediction that Paul had finished. He had not; he only called
for a few minutes' rest. About an hour later Paul began again. And
as before, he spoke not to the individual but to all in the church.

Therefore I, a prisoner for serving the Lord, beg you to
lead a life worthy of your calling, for you have been
called by God. Be humble and gentle. Be patient with
each other, making allowance for each other's faults because of your love. Always keep yourselves united in the
Holy Spirit, and bind yourselves together with peace.

Paul paused and said, "I must explain clearly about gifts to
these churches in eastern Asia Minor, or they will end up like
the church in Corinth, which is *too* gifted.
"I would to God that men did not make so much of gifts.
Gifts in the church are nothing but the gifts with which God
gifted his Son. The Son made nothing of his gifts. He gives gifts
for the church. They are not something to brag about!"

We are all one body, we have the same Spirit, and we
have all been called to the same glorious future. There
is only one Lord, one faith, one baptism, and there is
only one God and Father, who is over us all and in us all
and living through us all. However, he has given each
one of us a special gift according to the generosity of
Christ. That is why the Scriptures say,

> *"When he ascended to the heights,*
> *he led a crowd of captives*
> *and gave gifts to his people."*

Notice that it says "he ascended." This means that Christ first came down to the lowly world in which we live. The same one who came down is the one who ascended higher than all the heavens, so that his rule might fill the entire universe.

He is the one who gave these gifts to the church: the apostles, the prophets, the evangelists, and the pastors and teachers. Their responsibility is to equip God's people to do his work and build up the church, the body of Christ, until we come to such unity in our faith and knowledge of God's Son that we will be mature and full grown in the Lord, measuring up to the full stature of Christ.

"And when we reach full stature we will pour our lives out on the members of the church, the body of Christ! We will never boast of a gift, nor call attention to it. The first is strutting, the other is childish."

Then we will no longer be like children, forever changing our minds about what we believe because someone has told us something different or because someone has cleverly lied to us and made the lie sound like the truth.

Paul looked up at Timothy and then Epaphras. "I have seen this: men strong in the Lord until someone comes to them and talks them into believing something less is better. No one, no matter what he has to offer, can give the love that Christ—and the redeemed—can give. There is no safer place in creation than to be *in* Christ, *in* the community of his body."

Paul motioned Timothy to continue.

Instead, we will hold to the truth in love, becoming more and more in every way like Christ, who is the head of his body, the church. Under his direction, the whole body is fitted together perfectly. As each part does its own special work, it helps the other parts grow, so that the whole body is healthy and growing and full of love.

"Now I will get a little more serious with my words. You Gentiles—" Paul glanced at Epaphras—"sometimes have difficulty believing there is such a thing as moral decency."

With the Lord's authority let me say this: Live no longer as the ungodly do, for they are hopelessly confused. Their closed minds are full of darkness; they are far away from the life of God because they have shut their minds and hardened their hearts against him. They don't care anymore about right and wrong, and they have given themselves over to immoral ways. Their lives are filled with all kinds of impurity and greed.

But that isn't what you were taught when you learned about Christ. Since you have heard all about him and have learned the truth that is in Jesus, throw off your old evil nature and your former way of life, which is rotten through and through, full of lust and deception. Instead, there must be a spiritual renewal of your thoughts and attitudes. You must display a new nature because you are a new person, created in God's likeness—righteous, holy, and true.

So put away all falsehood and "tell your neighbor the truth" because we belong to each other. And "don't sin by letting anger gain control over you." Don't let the sun go down while you are still angry, for anger gives a mighty foothold to the Devil.

Paul then became even more specific. It was his way. Paul *always* ended his letters with practical exhortations.

If you are a thief, stop stealing. Begin using your hands for honest work, and then give generously to others in need. Don't use foul or abusive language. Let everything you say be good and helpful, so that your words will be an encouragement to those who hear them.

And do not bring sorrow to God's Holy Spirit by the way you live. Remember, he is the one who has identified you as his own, guaranteeing that you will be saved on the day of redemption.

Get rid of all bitterness, rage, anger, harsh words, and slander, as well as all types of malicious behavior. Instead, be kind to each other, tenderhearted, forgiving one another, just as God through Christ has forgiven you.

Paul was drawing on a lifetime of experience dealing with God's people. He knew firsthand how thoughtless Christians could sometimes be with other Christians . . . and with the people of the world.

Follow God's example in everything you do, because you are his dear children. Live a life filled with love for others, following the example of Christ, who loved you and gave himself as a sacrifice to take away your sins. And God was pleased, because that sacrifice was like sweet perfume to him.

Epaphras, who was becoming very impressed with Paul's words, was nonetheless stunned as he heard Paul speak bluntly and specifically about the deeds of the flesh.

Let there be no sexual immorality, impurity, or greed among you. Such sins have no place among God's people. Obscene stories, foolish talk, and coarse jokes—

these are not for you. Instead, let there be thankfulness to God. You can be sure that no immoral, impure, or greedy person will inherit the Kingdom of Christ and of God. For a greedy person is really an idolater who worships the things of this world. Don't be fooled by those who try to excuse these sins, for the terrible anger of God comes upon all those who disobey him. Don't participate in the things these people do. For though your hearts were once full of darkness, now you are full of light from the Lord, and your behavior should show it! For this light within you produces only what is good and right and true.

Try to find out what is pleasing to the Lord. Take no part in the worthless deeds of evil and darkness; instead, rebuke and expose them. It is shameful even to talk about the things that ungodly people do in secret. But when the light shines on them, it becomes clear how evil these things are. And where your light shines, it will expose their evil deeds. This is why it is said,

"Awake, O sleeper,
rise up from the dead,
and Christ will give you light."

So be careful how you live, not as fools but as those who are wise. Make the most of every opportunity for doing good in these evil days. Don't act thoughtlessly, but try to understand what the Lord wants you to do. Don't be drunk with wine, because that will ruin your life. Instead, let the Holy Spirit fill and control you. Then you will sing psalms and hymns and spiritual songs among yourselves, making music to the Lord in your hearts. And you will always give thanks for everything to God the Father in the name of our Lord Jesus Christ.

Paul reflected for a moment. He was asking himself what he might have left out and what more should be added. "Oh, how could I forget *this?*" he exclaimed.

And further, you will submit to one another out of reverence for Christ. You wives will submit to your husbands as you do to the Lord. For a husband is the head of his wife as Christ is the head of his body, the church; he gave his life to be her Savior. As the church submits to Christ, so you wives must submit to your husbands in everything.

And you husbands must love your wives with the same love Christ showed the church. He gave up his life for her to make her holy and clean, washed by baptism and God's word. He did this to present her to himself as a glorious church without a spot or wrinkle or any other blemish. Instead, she will be holy and without fault. In the same way, husbands ought to love their wives as they love their own bodies. For a man is actually loving himself when he loves his wife. No one hates his own body but lovingly cares for it, just as Christ cares for his body, which is the church. And we are his body.

As the Scriptures say, "A man leaves his father and mother and is joined to his wife, and the two are united into one." This is a great mystery, but it is an illustration of the way Christ and the church are one. So again I say, each man must love his wife as he loves himself, and the wife must respect her husband.

Children, obey your parents because you belong to the Lord, for this is the right thing to do. "Honor your father and mother." This is the first of the Ten Commandments that ends with a promise. And this is the promise: If you honor your father and mother, "you will live a long life, full of blessing." And now a word to you fathers. Don't make your children angry by the way you treat them. Rather, bring them up with the discipline and instruction approved by the Lord.

Timothy sensed Paul was about to end this part of his letter and move on to another topic. "Paul, a word to slaves. That is one half of the population of the Roman Empire."

Paul grimaced at a thought he would rather forget:

Slaves, obey your earthly masters with deep respect and fear. Serve them sincerely as you would serve Christ. Work hard, but not just to please your masters when they are watching. As slaves of Christ, do the will of God with all your heart. Work with enthusiasm, as though you were working for the Lord rather than for people. Remember that the Lord will reward each one of us for the good we do, whether we are slaves or free.

"Timothy, *you* forgot the *masters* of the slaves." Timothy ducked his head.

And in the same way, you masters must treat your slaves right. Don't threaten them; remember, you both have the same Master in heaven, and he has no favorites.

Paul paused a moment in thought and added encouraging spiritual advice for the church.

A final word: Be strong with the Lord's mighty power. Put on all of God's armor so that you will be able to stand firm against all strategies and tricks of the Devil. For we are not fighting against people made of flesh and blood, but against the evil rulers and authorities of the unseen world, against those mighty powers of darkness who rule this world, and against wicked spirits in the heavenly realms.

Use every piece of God's armor to resist the enemy in the time of evil, so that after the battle you will still be standing firm. Stand your ground, putting on the sturdy belt of truth and the body armor of God's righteousness. For shoes, put on the peace that comes from the Good News, so that you will be fully prepared. In every battle you will need faith as your shield to stop the fiery arrows aimed at you by Satan. Put on salvation as your helmet, and take the sword of the Spirit, which is the word of God. Pray at all times and on every occasion in the power of the Holy Spirit. Stay alert and be persistent in your prayers for all Christians everywhere.

It takes no imagination to understand Paul's next words. He was, after all, facing the possibility of being beheaded.

And pray for me, too. Ask God to give me the right words as I boldly explain God's secret plan that the Good News is for the Gentiles, too. I am in chains now for preaching this message as God's ambassador. But pray that I will keep on speaking boldly for him, as I should.

(Except for the closing benediction, the letter ended here; but later, when Epaphras became desperately ill, Paul added a word, explaining who would deliver this letter.)

Tychicus, a much loved brother and faithful helper in the Lord's work, will tell you all about how I am getting along. I am sending him to you for just this purpose. He will let you know how we are, and he will encourage you.

May God give you peace, dear brothers and sisters, and love with faith, from God the Father and the Lord Jesus Christ. May God's grace be upon all who love our Lord Jesus Christ with an undying love.

I, Gaius, implore you, as you read this letter, to keep in mind that both letters written to eastern Asia Minor were written to *churches*. These letters can be truly understood and experienced only in a community of believers. From Paul's view, the Christian walk only works in the context of the corporate assembly. He made it clear that our individual walk is held together and made possible only as we are in the community of the believers.

I add this personal word. There really is no such thing as living out the Christian life except it be lived *within* the ecclesia.

Now, there came a sudden change of events.

Even as Paul was putting down his pen, Epaphras was becoming ill.

Luke immediately came to Epaphras's side, but Epaphras was already losing consciousness. His breathing was an enormous struggle.

"I have listened to his chest: his lungs are filled with water. No man can survive long with a fever this high," Luke confided to Paul. "I know of nothing I can do for him." Luke shook his head sadly. "Brother Paul, prepare for the worst. This does not look good."

"If we lose Epaphras," said Paul, very quietly and very slowly, "we have lost the best we have."

Quite frankly, almost every person who gazed upon Epaphras expected him to die.

Who would carry greetings to Philippi and the other churches in northern Greece? Who would then go on to Asia Minor, to Colosse? Who would take Epaphras's place? Who would deliver these two letters to Colosse? (The man whom Paul chose—Tychicus—could not have been more surprised.)

CHAPTER 11

It will be the prayers of the church, and the churches, that will save him," sighed Paul gravely as he looked upon Epaphras's feverish body.

So began a long vigil. Night and day there was always someone beside Epaphras, praying for him. The church in Rome began an all-day and all-night vigil.

Epaphras, it turned out, was a strong man indeed. He simply refused to die, but neither could he recover. The disease that had come upon him refused to let go. The worst times were when Epaphras seemed to show improvement and then slipped back to the edge of death.

Paul could wait no longer. He finally called in Tychicus.

"If the fever should break even today, Epaphras would still be too weak to travel for months. It is growing late in the sailing season. I do not wish to subject him, or anyone, to the possibility of the Etesian winds. I have here two letters. They need to be delivered immediately. Tychicus, I turn to you. You know the dialects spoken in Colosse, and you also know Latin. I want you to leave here immediately with these letters."

Tychicus was surprised, to say the least. "Me! Why not...?"

"Why not *who?*" retorted Paul. "Secundus and Aristarchus are Greeks from Greece! *You* know Asia Minor and speak its language, and you know Latin."

"But Colossians speak Greek," protested Tychicus.

"Yes, but Philippians speak *Latin*," said Paul, smiling.

"You want me to go to Philippi, too! Please, let someone else go with me!" replied a slightly frightened Tychicus. "Philippi!" he repeated, obviously considering the quality of that ecclesia. "Me in Philippi . . . alone?"

"Exactly!" exclaimed Paul. "You learn quickly."

"Oh," was Tychicus's only response.

"Spend at least a month with my beloved Philippian Greeks. Tell them Epaphroditus is seriously ill. As soon as I know his fate, I will dispatch a letter to them.

"After you leave Philippi, cross the Aegean Sea. Go straight to Ephesus. Spend a few weeks with the church there."

"Me? Colosse! Philippi! *And Ephesus!* Paul, who do you think I am?"

As was his custom, Paul ignored Tychicus's comment.

"Give Ephesus a full report on my imprisonment. Leave copies of these two letters. Tell them to make more copies, and have them send the copies out to every assembly in Asia Minor. Tell the brothers and sisters in Ephesus to send word to those in every assembly that they should consider these two letters to be their very own. Then, Tychicus, having done that, make your way to Colosse. It is ninety miles east of Ephesus. I want you to remain in Colosse as long as you feel it is good. Spend a good deal of time with each of those three assemblies.

"If Philemon should seek out my view of Onesimus, tell Philemon that I *adore* Onesimus!" Paul stopped, then chuckled and added, "That should give Philemon pause as he considers Onesimus's fate. Then tell him I will send Onesimus home by way of Ephesus when Epaphras recovers."

"And if Epaphras should die?" queried Tychicus.

"Hmmm . . . then tell Philemon *I* will escort Onesimus back to Colosse if *I* do not die!"

"What if Philemon asks me what you think should be done with Onesimus?" responded Tychicus.

"You will have to guess, will you not, Tychicus?" Paul said, staring straight into his eyes. Tychicus, not knowing exactly what was going on, became nervous. Then it dawned on him what Paul was doing. He began to laugh.

He then turned away from Paul's burning gaze. "Yes, I will have to guess what you think Philemon should do with Onesimus. I will make a very, very *good* guess."

"Excellent. Now, leave immediately for Puteoli, and find a ship bound for Philippi. There are hundreds and hundreds of ships in that port, one of them must surely be on its way to Philippi."

"Paul, please tell me why I cannot take Trophimus with me."

"I wish Trophimus to remain here until I stand before Nero. I have asked that Luke also remain with me, as well as Aristarchus. If I am put to death, these men must be here to comfort the assembly. If I live, I want them to send word immediately across the empire, even as far as Jerusalem—in fact, even to Blastinius—that Paul lives!

"Before you go, I need to change the last paragraph of the letter I just finished. I need to tell those in Colosse, Hierapolis, and Laodicea that you will carry the letters to them."

Tychicus groaned. "They were expecting Epaphras!"

With the fate of Epaphras still uncertain, Tychicus departed Rome. When Tychicus set out, he did so with the fervent prayers of the church, asking their Lord that Tychicus be granted a good journey. They also asked God to soften Philemon's heart toward Onesimus.

And what did happen to Epaphras?

CHAPTER 12

For several more weeks Epaphras had an intermittent fever. Luke would say nothing about his chance of recovery until the fever had completely departed and several more days had passed.

Finally Luke rendered a verdict. "Epaphras will recover. But he must have rest; he will have no strength for weeks. A body cannot take what that brother has been through and recover quickly."

Everyone rejoiced at the news. All the believers in Rome had come to love this man who had ministered and served so brilliantly for Christ and whose life backed up every word he preached.

Interestingly, for a while it slipped Paul's mind to send a letter to the assembly in Philippi to let them know that Epaphras had *not* died.

In the meantime, Tychicus was making his way to Philippi. Upon his arrival, he could only tell the church in Philippi: "Epaphras is gravely ill. Whether he will live or die I do not know."

The Philippian Christians could not take this uncertainty. A messenger from the church was dispatched to Rome, along with *dozens* of letters to be delivered to Epaphras, *if* he was still alive.

Shortly thereafter the messenger arrived in Rome.

Priscilla stood at the door listening to the Philippian messenger's inquiry about Epaphras's condition. "Oh, my," was her only speech. Taking the man by the hand, she immediately led him through the maze of Roman streets to Paul's room, there to present Epaphras . . . alive.

"It appears you have an urgent letter from the Philippians. I cannot but wonder why they sent a messenger! Do you know?" she asked Paul coolly.

Paul turned red. He greeted the messenger with an apology. The messenger, in turn, handed a letter to Paul, then dismissed himself. Paul pulled Epaphras aside and began sharing with him the many greetings that had come from Philippi.

"There is something curious about this letter," observed Paul.

"Actually, Paul, there are two letters," Priscilla pointed out.

"The messenger has come all the way from Philippi, his expenses paid by the assembly there; I perceive the hand of someone who deals in purple cloth," he said, his face breaking into a pleased smile. "And letters are not all he brought," Paul added.

"A gift again!" said Priscilla.

"Yes. But why two letters?" asked Paul as he handed the two scrolls to Priscilla.

"One is from Tychicus; the other is from the entire assembly. Both letters," said Priscilla as she glanced at their contents, "ask the same question.

"The church is well. Ah, Tychicus does say there are two sisters who are at odds with one another. It is not a great problem, Tychicus says, but it is a nagging one."

Paul nodded. "I have had many of those kinds of problems," he sighed.

"Now the other letter," said Priscilla, as she mulled over a much longer letter. "This letter is mostly inquiring about Epaphras."

Priscilla looked up. "Paul! They are so concerned about

Epaphras. It is so unfortunate that you forgot to write Philippi and tell them whether or not Epaphras is alive or dead!"

Paul was about to apologize again when Priscilla continued, "I also forgot."

Paul put his hand to his forehead. "I must get a letter off to Philippi immediately. In the meantime, Priscilla, would you tell this dear brother from Philippi all you can about what has happened since I arrived in Rome?

"Aristarchus," said Paul, turning to his Thessalonian friend, "go next door. Ask Epaphras and the messenger to come here. Find Luke, and the two of you spend as much time with this Philippian as you can. When he returns home to Philippi, I wish him to be able to answer any possible questions he is going to be asked. Most of all, I want him to tell the assembly of God in Philippi that the assembly that gathers here in Rome is growing in number."

A few moments later an ebullient Epaphras and a gleeful messenger came, arm in arm, into Paul's room.

"You must write a letter to Philippi," said the brother from Greece.

"I know, and I will," responded Paul. "But I have two letters to write, one to comfort a church, the other to save a young man from execution. Which shall I write first?"

"Oh," replied Epaphras. "Onesimus *is* returning to Colosse to face Philemon. Please, Paul, write Philemon first. Take all the time you need. That letter is terribly important. *Then* write Philippi."

"I am quite ready to write a letter to Philemon! I have given a great deal of thought as to how to form this letter. It must be penned in such a way that leaves Philemon *no* room to execute Onesimus."

Here, then, is not only one of the most interesting letters one man ever penned to another, but if you look closely, you will see just how clever Paul could be in dealing with major crises.

CHAPTER 13

Epaphras, I am about to send a brief letter to Philemon. You and Onesimus begin your final preparation for leaving Italy and going back to Colosse. You must not only visit Philippi, but you must also stay there for a good while."

Paul turned to the young slave who had waited on him day and night for over six months and become so dear to him. "Onesimus, you will accompany Epaphroditus to Philippi, but once there, you must go on home to Colosse . . . and to the home of Philemon."

"I am dead," groaned Onesimus as he dropped to the floor.

"Perhaps, but I am writing a letter to Philemon on your behalf, which may save your life."

"Will it do any good? Philemon wants me dead. I know. I stole from him, and you do not steal from Philemon."

"I agree. He is a hard businessman with whom I would not like to do business," Paul replied in a somber voice.

Onesimus began to cry. "I am dead. I know I am dead."

Timothy could not help but notice a slight smile on Paul's face. *He is up to something for certain*, thought Timothy.

"Leave me now, Onesimus. Timothy and I will write to Philemon this very hour. Tomorrow I will have you and

Epaphras read the letter. Go now, for this is a letter that needs to be written well."

Rising before Epaphras the next morning, Timothy was all smiles when he greeted Epaphras in Paul's room. "Where is Onesimus?" inquired Timothy.

"He fell asleep only a few minutes ago," responded Epaphras. "He did not sleep all night. I believe he has been thinking much about dying."

"A waste!" said Timothy with a laugh.

"Here is my letter to Philemon," said Paul, in a way that seemed to be detached from the seriousness of Onesimus's situation.

"Timothy, if you would please go to Epaphras's room and bring him here to me. After that, I will call in Onesimus."

A moment later Epaphras opened the scroll and read it with great hesitance. Epaphras read slowly and sometimes with great labor for, of the men trained in Ephesus, he had the least formal training. About halfway through the letter even Epaphras began to laugh, so hard, in fact, that he and Timothy embraced one another and laughed together.

"Oh, Paul, you have outdone yourself. Never, never, *never* have I read such a letter!" Epaphras finally managed to say.

Paul could not have been more pleased. "Will it help Onesimus?" asked Paul mischievously.

"Onesimus is the safest slave on earth! A pardon is at hand," countered Timothy, still laughing out of control.

The letter opened with a typical greeting from Paul. See if you can discern the reason for Timothy's cheerful outburst. (By the way, this letter later came to be known as "the letter of unveiled hints.")

This letter is from Paul, in prison for preaching the Good News about Christ Jesus, and from our brother Timothy.

It is written to Philemon, our much loved co-worker, and to our sister Apphia and to Archippus, a fellow soldier of the cross. I am also writing to the church that meets in your house.

May God our Father and the Lord Jesus Christ give you grace and peace.

I always thank God when I pray for you, Philemon, because I keep hearing of your trust in the Lord Jesus and your love for all of God's people. You are generous because of your faith. And I am praying that you will really put your generosity to work, for in so doing you will come to an understanding of all the good things we can do for Christ. I myself have gained much joy and comfort from your love, my brother, because your kindness has so often refreshed the hearts of God's people.

That is why I am boldly asking a favor of you. I could demand it in the name of Christ because it is the right thing for you to do, but because of our love, I prefer just to ask you. So take this as a request from your friend Paul, an old man, now in prison for the sake of Christ Jesus.

My plea is that you show kindness to Onesimus. I think of him as my own son . . .

(Paul had cast himself as both a father and mother to the Corinthians. And here Paul extends his fatherly affection to Philemon's slave.)

. . . because he became a believer as a result of my ministry here in prison. Onesimus hasn't been of much use to you in the past, but now he is very useful to both of us. I am sending him back to you, and with him comes my own heart.

I really wanted to keep him here with me while I am in these chains for preaching the Good News, and he would have helped me on your behalf. But I didn't want to do anything without your consent. And I didn't want you to help because you were forced to do it but because you wanted to. Perhaps you could think of it this way: Onesimus ran away for a little while so you could have him back forever. He is no longer just a slave; he is a beloved brother, especially to me. Now he will mean much more to you, both as a slave and as a brother in the Lord.

So if you consider me your partner, give him the same welcome you would give me if I were coming. If he has harmed you in any way or stolen anything from you, charge me for it. I, Paul, write this in my own handwriting: "I will repay it." And I won't mention that you owe me your very soul!

Yes, dear brother, please do me this favor for the Lord's sake. Give me this encouragement in Christ. I am confident as I write this letter that you will do what I ask and even more!

Please keep a guest room ready for me, for I am hoping that God will answer your prayers and let me return to you soon.

"Go wake up Onesimus and bring him in," said Paul, struggling to hide his pleasure.

Onesimus came in, his face ashen, his body trembling. Timothy read the letter to him. Onesimus, however, was so taken up with the certainty of his doom, that it was obvious he had not caught what Paul had done.

"Read it to him *again*," instructed Paul.

"What is Paul saying to Philemon? Is he telling Philemon to kill me?" asked Onesimus in all innocence.

Timothy responded: "There is much in the letter that Paul says. But, oh, it is what he *almost* says that is so outrageous."

"Huh?" responded Onesimus.

"In Greek your name, Onesimus, means 'useful.' Paul plays on the meaning of your name. But there is much more. For instance, Paul openly admits that you stole money from Philemon *and* that you, Onesimus, owe him a great deal."

"Oooh," groaned Onesimus.

"But then Paul *almost* says this: 'Philemon, I brought you to Christ. You, Philemon, owe me, Paul, much, much more than Onesimus owes you. So subtract what Onesimus owes you from what you owe me!'"

Timothy continued explaining, "Paul called Philemon generous. Then Paul hints to Philemon to let you go unpunished, which would be a generous thing to do for *Christ*. Then Paul says he needs a favor—but he hints to Philemon that he has a right to *demand* the favor. He tells Philemon that doing this favor is the only right thing Philemon can do. 'But no,' says Paul, 'because we love one another, and because I am very old and in chains, Philemon, I only *ask* the favor.'"

Epaphras began to laugh again.

"What is the favor?" blurted out Onesimus anxiously.

"To be *kind* to Onesimus!"

"Hallelujah!" cried Onesimus.

Timothy continued, "'Onesimus is like a son to me,' says Paul. Here Paul is hinting again: 'Philemon you would not want to kill *my son*, would you?'"

Onesimus came over to Paul and kissed him.

"Then Paul tells Philemon that you became a Christian. 'True, Onesimus has not been profitable to you, Philemon, but Onesimus is *profitable* to me, Paul.'"

"'Now,' says Paul, 'I am sending Onesimus home to you. But it is like sending you my *heart*.'"

Onesimus fell back and yelled, "I am not going to die!"

The three men watching Onesimus could not but roar with laughter.

"Ah, Onesimus, Paul has not even begun to save your hide. There is so much more he says in this letter. Paul says, 'I am sure you would have freely sent Onesimus to me here in Rome if you had known how much he would help me.

"'Onesimus isn't just a slave, Philemon, he is now your *brother*. And he is *my* brother.'"

"So you see," said Epaphras, interrupting Timothy, "you are now Paul's son and brother. Will Philemon hurt Paul's son and brother?"

Onesimus beamed. "I surely do not think so!"

"Wait until you hear this. *Then* Paul says to Philemon, 'Give Onesimus the same welcome you would give me— Paul!'"

Onesimus jumped up and began whirling around. "Me, greeted by Philemon as if *I* were Paul! Day of days!"

"Does he say, I mean, does he *hint* anything else?" asked Onesimus, as he held the letter up to the light.

"Paul says he expects Philemon to do all this . . . *and* more."

"What *more?*"

"You don't know?"

"No, I am a slave; I am not quick like you."

"When Paul says, 'I expect you, Philemon, to do even more than I ask,' he is hinting to Philemon to set you *free!*"

"No!" said a stunned Onesimus, as he sank to the floor. "No one would do that for *me!*"

"If you had any money, I would be sorely tempted to bet with you," roared Timothy.

"One more sentence, Onesimus. Paul asked Philemon to hold open a room for him . . . for Paul. Imagine Paul coming to Philemon's home, after a letter like this. Do you see Onesimus in any great danger?"

Very soberly Onesimus turned, tears coursing down his

very white skin. "No, I do not. I will be safe. Thanks to God, and the letter, and Paul, I *will* be safe."

Paul had watched this entire drama with a great deal of satisfaction. Now he interrupted with more surprises.

"Timothy, see to it that a good number of copies of this letter are made. Make sure Epaphras has several copies. Epaphras should leave one copy in Philippi. I have good reason to ask you to do so. Because you all know the dangers of the open seas, I want you to also send a copy to Ephesus and have them carry one to Colosse, one to Hierapolis, and, of course, one to Laodicea. I will not be unduly angry if someone reads this letter and shares its contents with others. I would not be too unhappy even if others see this letter *before* Philemon sees it."

"This has *nothing* to do with influencing Philemon, does it?" asked a straight-faced Timothy.

Ignoring Timothy's words, Paul spoke gently to Onesimus. "We will all be holding you up to the Lord as you return home. Now, if you will please once more be so kind as to leave me."

Paul turned to Timothy, "Epaphras and Onesimus will soon be among the beloved ones in Philippi. Epaphras must not only be accompanied by Onesimus, but he must also be carrying a letter from me.

"Timothy, you stay. Help me write a letter to the holy ones in Philippi."

And what a writing it was. And what a shock one part of that letter was to Epaphras!

CHAPTER 14

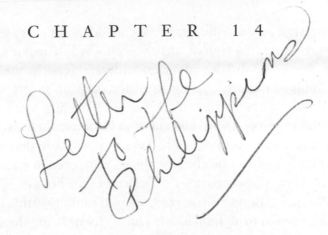

Letter to Philippians

What shall I say to my much-loved Philippians?" questioned Paul.

"Ah, Paul," responded Timothy enthusiastically, "tell them what you yourself have just learned: that believing Jews from Israel are pouring into Gentile churches everywhere. In your last two letters you have more or less told Gentile Christians to expect that a few Hebrews would try to convert Gentiles to obeying 613 laws. Maybe you should touch on this even to the Philippians."

"That I will do," said the man who had once been a Pharisee of Pharisees.

"Now, the one thing that troubles me most about the Philippian assembly is the dispute between Euodia and Syntyche. I am concerned that they, of all people, would be causing dissension."

"I share your concern," agreed Timothy. "Thank God and thanks to you the churches have *outside* workers to assist in settling *inside* disputes."

"Then let us begin. Do you have a pen?"

"I do," said Timothy, mumbling something about wishing Tertius were present.

The opening of the letter surprised all of us. For the first time *ever*, Paul made a reference to elders. In every letter Paul ever wrote to a church, that church was in a major crisis; yet, never once did he mention elders. Here is the beloved Philippian church, living in peace, and he mentions elders. True, the greeting to elders was but a passing word; still Paul had never *ever* mentioned elders in his letters to churches. Previously, Paul went out of his way to make sure that the entire church, and no one else, ran the church, even in crisis.

I now present to you Paul's letter to the body of believers in Philippi. Always, as you read, keep in mind that this letter was not written to an individual. The secret of living the Christian life always belongs *inside* the *corporate* body of believers.

This letter is from Paul and Timothy, slaves of Christ Jesus.

It is written to all of God's people in Philippi, who believe in Christ Jesus, and to the elders and deacons.

May God our Father and the Lord Jesus Christ give you grace and peace.

Paul stopped dictating and said, "Timothy, of the thirteen or fourteen churches which have come into existence through my hand, I must admit that the Philippians have a very special place in my life. Philippi has stood with me in my darkest hours and has helped me in the Lord's work, beyond all others. Write this":

Every time I think of you, I give thanks to my God. I always pray for you, and I make my requests with a heart full of joy because you have been my partners in spreading the Good News about Christ from the time you first heard it until now. And I am sure that God, who began the good work within you, will continue his work until it is finally finished on that day when Christ Jesus comes back again.

It is right that I should feel as I do about all of you, for you have a very special place in my heart. We have shared together the blessings of God, both when I was in prison and when I was out, defending the truth and telling others the Good News. God knows how much I love you and long for you with the tender compassion of Christ Jesus.

Musing aloud, Paul said, "There is so much peace in the assembly in Philippi. Compare them to Corinth. The holy ones in Corinth fight all the time. Philippi lives in peace. May it ever be."

I pray that your love for each other will overflow more and more, and that you will keep on growing in your knowledge and understanding. For I want you to understand what really matters, so that you may live pure and blameless lives until Christ returns. May you always be filled with the fruit of your salvation—those good things that are produced in your life by Jesus Christ—for this will bring much glory and praise to God.

"Philippi needs to know that my imprisonment here in Rome has turned out far beyond anything I hoped. The gospel has reached the palace of Nero. And because of you, Timothy, and the others from Ephesus preaching in the streets of Rome, now many other believers in the assembly have dared to follow your example."

And I want you to know, dear brothers and sisters, that everything that has happened to me here has helped to spread the Good News. For everyone here, including all the soldiers in the palace guard, knows that I am in

chains because of Christ. And because of my imprisonment, many of the Christians here have gained confidence and become more bold in telling others about
Christ.

Some are preaching out of jealousy and rivalry. But
others preach about Christ with pure motives. They
preach because they love me, for they know the Lord
brought me here to defend the Good News. Those others do not have pure motives as they preach about
Christ. They preach with selfish ambition, not sincerely, intending to make my chains more painful to
me. But whether or not their motives are pure, the fact
remains that the message about Christ is being
preached, so I rejoice. And I will continue to rejoice. For
I know that as you pray for me and as the Spirit of Jesus
Christ helps me, this will all turn out for my deliverance.

"The Philippians need to know how I feel about the pros-
pect of being beheaded here in Rome. In fact, everyone needs
to know."

For I live in eager expectation and hope that I will never
do anything that causes me shame, but that I will always
be bold for Christ, as I have been in the past, and that
my life will always honor Christ, whether I live or I die.
For to me, living is for Christ, and dying is even better.
Yet if I live, that means fruitful service for Christ. I really don't know which is better. I'm torn between two
desires: Sometimes I want to live, and sometimes I long
to go and be with Christ. That would be far better for
me, but it is better for you that I live.

I am convinced of this, so I will continue with you
so that you will grow and experience the joy of your
faith. Then when I return to you, you will have even

more reason to boast about what Christ Jesus has done for me.

But whatever happens to me, you must live in a manner worthy of the Good News about Christ, as citizens of heaven. Then, whether I come and see you again or only hear about you, I will know that you are standing side by side, fighting together for the Good News.

"Hmmm. If I die here, what *will* happen? How will God's people in Philippi react to my absence? Timothy, all of you must be strong. It will not be a time for fear or discouragement."

Don't be intimidated by your enemies. This will be a sign to them that they are going to be destroyed, but that you are going to be saved, even by God himself. For you have been given not only the privilege of trusting in Christ but also the privilege of suffering for him. We are in this fight together. You have seen me suffer for him in the past, and you know that I am still in the midst of this great struggle.

Is there any encouragement from belonging to Christ? Any comfort from his love? Any fellowship together in the Spirit? Are your hearts tender and sympathetic? Then make me truly happy by agreeing wholeheartedly with each other, loving one another, and working together with one heart and purpose.

"I did not, in the beginning, exhort and emphasize unity as much as I should have. Today, in my old age, I do not neglect this. God's people have shown me that Christians loving one another is not a guarantee. Christians do not always love one another.

"Right now, the churches don't need disunity."

Don't be selfish; don't live to make a good impression on others. Be humble, thinking of others as better than yourself. Don't think only about your own affairs, but be interested in others, too, and what they are doing.

Your attitude should be the same that Christ Jesus had. Though he was God, he did not demand and cling to his rights as God. He made himself nothing; he took the humble position of a slave and appeared in human form. And in human form he obediently humbled himself even further by dying a criminal's death on a cross. Because of this, God raised him up to the heights of heaven and gave him a name that is above every other name, so that at the name of Jesus every knee will bow, in heaven and on earth and under the earth, and every tongue will confess that Jesus Christ is Lord, to the glory of God the Father.

Dearest friends, you were always so careful to follow my instructions when I was with you. And now that I am away you must be even more careful to put into action God's saving work in your lives, obeying God with deep reverence and fear. For God is working in you, giving you the desire to obey him and the power to do what pleases him.

"Paul, you have been speaking of problems of conflict *in* an assembly. This problem is just as great outside the assembly," Timothy said.

In everything you do, stay away from complaining and arguing, so that no one can speak a word of blame against you. You are to live clean, innocent lives as children of God in a dark world full of crooked and perverse people. Let your lives shine brightly before them.

Paul paused. His mind wandered into the future. He then spoke his thoughts.

Hold tightly to the word of life, so that when Christ returns, I will be proud that I did not lose the race and that my work was not useless. But even if my life is to be poured out like a drink offering to complete the sacrifice of your faithful service (that is, if I am to die for you), I will rejoice, and I want to share my joy with all of you. And you should be happy about this and rejoice with me.

"Tychicus left here several months ago and reported to Philippi, telling them of my situation here in Rome. He then went on to Colosse with the two letters I wrote them.

"Timothy, Philippi is now expecting you to come to them.

"Over in Colosse they are expecting Epaphras. This seems simple enough, except for one problem. I need you here—*here* until Nero decides my fate. As you know, I have great confidence in Epaphras. I am sending him to Greece and then, later, to Colosse and Laodicea. Perhaps after I stand before Nero, I will send you to Philippi. It is time I told the Philippians this. Epaphras is already much loved in Philippi. They will be pleased."

If the Lord Jesus is willing, I hope to send Timothy to you soon. Then when he comes back, he can cheer me up by telling me how you are getting along. I have no one else like Timothy, who genuinely cares about your welfare. All the others care only for themselves and not for what matters to Jesus Christ. But you know how Timothy has proved himself. Like a son with his father, he has helped me in preaching the Good News. I hope to send him to you just as soon as I find out what is going to happen to me here. And I have confidence from the Lord that I myself will come to see you soon.

Meanwhile, I thought I should send Epaphroditus back to you. He is a true brother, a faithful worker, and a courageous soldier. And he was your [apostle] to help me in my need. Now I am sending him home again, for he has been longing to see you, and he was very distressed that you heard he was ill. And he surely was ill; in fact, he almost died. But God had mercy on him—and also on me, so that I would not have such unbearable sorrow.

So I am all the more anxious to send him back to you, for I know you will be glad to see him, and that will lighten all my cares. Welcome him with Christian love and with great joy, and be sure to honor people like him. For he risked his life for the work of Christ, and he was at the point of death while trying to do for me the things you couldn't do because you were far away.

Whatever happens, dear brothers and sisters, may the Lord give you joy. I never get tired of telling you this. I am doing this for your own good.

"In almost every letter I have written I have had something to say about the party of the circumcised." Paul's eyes twinkled as he said, "I am too old to change now."

Watch out for those dogs, those wicked men and their evil deeds, those mutilators who say you must be circumcised to be saved. For we who worship God in the Spirit are the only ones who are truly circumcised. We put no confidence in human effort. Instead, we boast about what Christ Jesus has done for us.

Yet I could have confidence in myself if anyone

could. If others have reason for confidence in their own efforts, I have even more! For I was circumcised when I was eight days old, having been born into a pure-blooded Jewish family that is a branch of the tribe of Benjamin. So I am a real Jew if there ever was one! What's more, I was a member of the Pharisees, who demand the strictest obedience to the Jewish law. And zealous? Yes, in fact, I harshly persecuted the church. And I obeyed the Jewish law so carefully that I was never accused of any fault.

I once thought all these things were so very important, but now I consider them worthless because of what Christ has done. Yes, everything else is worthless when compared with the priceless gain of knowing Christ Jesus my Lord. I have discarded everything else, counting it all as garbage, so that I may have Christ and become one with him. I no longer count on my own goodness or my ability to obey God's law, but I trust Christ to save me. For God's way of making us right with himself depends on faith. As a result, I can really know Christ and experience the mighty power that raised him from the dead. I can learn what it means to suffer with him, sharing in his death, so that, somehow, I can experience the resurrection from the dead!

I don't mean to say that I have already achieved these things or that I have already reached perfection! But I keep working toward that day when I will finally be all that Christ Jesus saved me for and wants me to be. No, dear brothers and sisters, I am still not all I should be, but I am focusing all my energies on this one thing: Forgetting the past and looking forward to what lies ahead, I strain to reach the end of the race and receive the prize for which God, through Christ Jesus, is calling us up to heaven.

"That was clear," said Timothy. "When the hour comes, I trust Philippi will remember your words if Judaizers arrive in Philippi again." Paul nodded and continued:

I hope all of you who are mature Christians will agree on these things. If you disagree on some point, I believe God will make it plain to you. But we must be sure to obey the truth we have learned already.

Paul began pouring out his heart. Timothy could hardly keep up.

Dear brothers and sisters, pattern your lives after mine, and learn from those who follow our example. For I have told you often before, and I say it again with tears in my eyes, that there are many whose conduct shows they are really enemies of the cross of Christ. Their future is eternal destruction. Their god is their appetite, they brag about shameful things, and all they think about is this life here on earth. But we are citizens of heaven, where the Lord Jesus Christ lives. And we are eagerly waiting for him to return as our Savior. He will take these weak mortal bodies of ours and change them into glorious bodies like his own, using the same mighty power that he will use to conquer everything, everywhere.

Dear brothers and sisters, I love you and long to see you, for you are my joy and the reward for my work. So please stay true to the Lord, my dear friends.

Paul stopped. "Now to the matter of Euodia and Syntyche. It's time to say something before their quarrel becomes a serious problem."

And now I want to plead with those two women, Euodia and Syntyche. Please, because you belong to the Lord, settle your disagreement. And I ask you, my true team-mate, to help these women, for they worked hard with me in telling others the Good News. And they worked with Clement and the rest of my co-workers, whose names are written in the Book of Life.

I, Gaius, have often read Paul's letter to the Philippian church. The next few lines are among the most beautiful Paul ever wrote to a church.

Always be full of joy in the Lord. I say it again—rejoice! Let everyone see that you are considerate in all you do. Remember, the Lord is coming soon.
Don't worry about anything; instead, pray about everything. Tell God what you need, and thank him for all he has done. If you do this, you will experience God's peace, which is far more wonderful than the human mind can understand. His peace will guard your hearts and minds as you live in Christ Jesus.

Timothy knew instinctively Paul was closing his letter, but the words of beautiful exhortations continued.

And now, dear brothers and sisters, let me say one more thing as I close this letter. Fix your thoughts on what is true and honorable and right. Think about things that are pure and lovely and admirable. Think about things that are excellent and worthy of praise. Keep putting into practice all you learned from me and heard from me and saw me doing, and the God of peace will be with you.

Paul reached back into his memory and once again recalled how much Philippi had helped him—and was still helping him.

How grateful I am, and how I praise the Lord that you are concerned about me again. I know you have always been concerned for me, but for a while you didn't have the chance to help me. Not that I was ever in need, for I have learned how to get along happily whether I have much or little. I know how to live on almost nothing or with everything. I have learned the secret of living in every situation, whether it is with a full stomach or empty, with plenty or little. For I can do everything with the help of Christ who gives me the strength I need. But even so, you have done well to share with me in my present difficulty.

As you know, you Philippians were the only ones who gave me financial help when I brought you the Good News and then traveled on from Macedonia. No other church did this.

Tears ran down Timothy's face as he recalled how Paul and Silas were almost starving in Greece when an incredibly large gift arrived from the assembly in Philippi.

Even when I was in Thessalonica you sent help more than once. I don't say this because I want a gift from you. What I want is for you to receive a well-earned reward because of your kindness.

At the moment I have all I need—more than I need! I am generously supplied with the gifts you sent me with Epaphroditus. They are a sweet-smelling sacrifice that is acceptable to God and pleases him. And this same God who takes care of me will supply all your needs from his glorious riches, which have been given to us in Christ Jesus. Now glory be to God our Father forever and ever. Amen.

When the letter was finished, Paul handed it to Epaphras. "Please read it. This letter is what you will deliver to the believers in Philippi."

Epaphras was astounded to be referred to by Paul as a "sent one," that is, an apostle. Yet, there it was, clearly written in Greek:

> Consider Epaphroditus, my brother and my coworker
> and fellow soldier, to be *your* apostle.

A few days later Epaphras and a not-so-fearful Onesimus set out for Philippi.

Whenever Nero decided Paul's fate, Paul wanted word to go forth to Greece and Ephesus. He decided Ephesus would receive the news by Tychicus. Eastern Asia Minor would hear by means of Trophimus. Antioch would hear by way of Titus. Thessalonica and Berea would hear by means of Secundus.

John Mark, Luke, and Timothy would stay in Rome until after the trial. Then, no matter what the decision was, Mark would leave Italy, search out Peter, and report to him about Nero's decision.

Regardless of the outcome, Aristarchus was to remain in Rome (a decision that, unwittingly, later cost him his life).

It is now time to recount to you the day Paul faced Nero and the outcome of that day.

CHAPTER 15

It was the middle of the night. Priscilla, accompanied by two Roman soldiers, made her way through the streets of Rome until she came to the house where Paul lived. As soon as Paul opened his eyes, Priscilla spoke. "Paul, you will stand before Nero in one week." Paul sat up.

"How do you know?"

"I know," said Priscilla, always a little mysterious about her relationship to Caesar's palace and the influential people of Rome.

"We must speak of many things," she continued. "I will return tomorrow. In the meantime, I will alert the gathering."

"How did you come to have Roman guards accompany you in the middle of the night? Roman guards do not do that."

"These did," replied Priscilla as she turned and left the room.

The next day Paul and Priscilla talked for many long hours.

"Paul, keep in mind Nero was sixteen when he rose to the throne. Seneca and Burrus really ruled until Nero deposed Seneca, and Burrus died of throat cancer.

"Nero also disposed of his mother, Agrippina. He had her killed. He was estranged from his wife, Octavia. When she was about to bear his child, he kicked her to death. Since then, he has had a mistress named Poppaea. The blood of mad Caligula is surfacing. Now, at age twenty-two, he firmly thinks he is a god. He is drawing up plans for a vast garden, a palace unsurpassed in human history, and a bronze statue larger than any ever cast.

"As to the empire, Pax Romana holds, but the fabric is tearing everywhere."

On and on they talked. The next day Priscilla seemed to disappear. She was calling in every favor owed her.

Priscilla returned just two days before the trial. "Paul, Nero has little interest in being emperor. He believes that he is a great artist. To rule the empire, for him, is but a necessary and inconvenient means for pursuing his artistic ability.

"I did not know this, but the people close to him tell me he has already secretly performed as singer and poet to small, private groups in Neapolis. They have fed his blind ego with false and extravagant praise. He seems to have convinced himself he is one of the greatest singers, poets, philosophers and, alas, athletes of all times.

"At best, Nero is poor at all of these. He has made a fool of himself. When you meet him, if you do, you will meet a fat, dissipated, egomaniac who truly believes he is an Olympian god. Keep all this in mind. There is one good omen—you will have only one hearing. This almost always means you will be freed. Men who are certain to die always are given two hearings. You will be asked a few questions in the presence of a few jurists. Some will be harsh; their purpose is to intimidate you. Some will be conciliatory—unless your guilt is assured. Then there will be no conciliatory questions."

The very next day, just before he would appear at Caesar's palace, Paul was visited by some of Nero's underlings, who explained to Paul exactly what the ritual of appearing before Nero would be like.

"You will be taken to the palace by armed guards. Your clothes will be taken from you, and you will be dressed in fine apparel. You will probably spend one or two nights in the palace awaiting your trial."

Paul listened quietly. He felt confident this group of imperial advocates would see this charge for what it was, a question of religious views. If so, the court would probably not be inclined to get involved in religious disputes.

Paul had only one question. He had been asking Priscilla and all his visitors the same question he was about to ask these royal advocates: "Will I see Nero? Can I make my appeal directly to him?"

The gruff answer was: "What insolence! You, a common Jew, wishing to take time out of the life of the great Caesar? It is out of the question."

What everyone, including Nero, had not counted on was Priscilla. By now she had spoken to virtually every powerful person in Rome. Nor did any of the believers have any idea of the influence that this very determined woman could exert. The extent of Priscilla's influence emerged when it was discovered that *she* had been given the right to appear with Paul before Caesar. Everyone, including the court, was astonished.

In the morning, guards in full parade dress appeared outside Paul's room. From there he was taken through the streets with fifes and drums into the imperial palace. This particular palace had been built years before by the second Caesar, Augustus.

As Paul had been told, he was given new garments, Roman in fashion. Paul protested. He wanted to stand before Nero in the garb of a Pharisee. It was not to be so. And, yes, Paul did spend the night in the palace. Paul assumed he would be heard early in the morning of the next day. Instead, he waited all day and late into the evening before any attention was given to him.

Nero did not usually awaken until late afternoon.

(There were stories that circulate even now that early in his reign, Nero roamed the streets of Rome at night with a small contingency of soldiers, all of them dressed in the garb of thieves. There, the story goes, he fell on innocent prey, beat them senseless, and robbed them.)

Late in the night Roman soldiers came to Paul's cell and marched him before the advocates and magistrates. Just then Priscilla, dressed in royal garments, took her place beside Paul. Priscilla was not unknown to this court, nor was her royal standing to be dismissed.

A few hard questions were asked. Then a few conciliatory ones. A moment came when the tension eased. One of the jurists remarked, "I have sat here for over ten years, and rarely have I ever seen so much effort exerted to assure this court that the man who stands before us is innocent."

The court was about to render its verdict when the emperor was heard speaking with some foreign dignitary. Nero was describing the garden he planned, comparing it with the Hanging Gardens of Babylon.

"And a bronze statue of me at its entrance, ninety feet tall, taller than the Colossus of Alexander, and a palace to shame any the world has ever seen."

The jurists stood. Someone announced: "The god Nero!"

When Paul and Nero met, Nero was not yet twenty-three; Paul was in his mid-fifties. Be assured, though, that Paul looked far older than that.

(In exactly six years both men would be dead. In just eight years, both Jerusalem and its temple would be destroyed.)

Nero swaggered into the room. Astonishingly, his first words were a greeting. "Ah, the Lady Priscilla." Priscilla bowed and addressed Nero in the local dialect of the city, one used only by friends.

Even Paul was stunned at seeing Priscilla in royal garb and so comfortable in this palatial setting.

Nero was a stout man with a completely round face. Every

hair on his head seemed to be at war with the others. His complexion was not that of the typical Italian. His skin was light, his neck nonexistent, his eyes, as Priscilla had said, were blue.

Nero's degenerate living was already manifesting itself. His face was puffy, his eyes swollen, his notorious overeating obvious.

Paul could not help but think, *The bronze makers will certainly not show his physique the way I am now seeing it.*

"Is this the Jew?" asked Nero, his voice revealing virtually no interest. "The one my court has heard so much about?"

"It is," said one of the magistrates, as he bowed low.

What you may find to be amazing is that Nero already knew a great deal about Christians and that there were some in Rome. Perhaps more important, he understood Christians were to be distinguished from the Jewish religion. How was this possible when there were fewer than three hundred Christians in all of Rome? Once more we find our answer in Priscilla. By her influence, a number of believers had been hired to serve in Nero's household. (It is a truism that the closer you are to power, the more influence you have.)

Consequently, Christians were crossing Nero's pathway every day. On several occasions these simple servants found themselves totally alone in Nero's presence and there told him of their faith. Nero's interest, his *only* interest, was based on his superstitious nature, and that, in turn, centered on one subject: power. (Nero was curious about only one thing—how it came to be that a man could raise himself from the dead. On occasion, then, Nero made inquiries of the Christians about this "god" named Jesus.)

Paul opened his mouth to speak, keenly aware this was the one person in the entire world to whom he most wanted to give his testimony. If Paul could make inroads into the palace, the future of the faith might be more secure. Paul's diligent prayer had been that he might gain Nero's sympathy for believers in Christ and, perhaps—he dared believe—that he might even bring him to salvation in Christ.

But Paul had utterly underestimated the depravity of this man.

"I am Paul of Tarsus, a Hebrew and a Roman."

Nero was paying no attention. "Your God, did he rise from the dead as they say? If so, where is he?"

"My Lord, whose name is Jesus Christ, is alive. I met him on the road to Damascus, where he appeared to me in a bright light."

"Then where is he?" urged Nero gruffly.

"He has ascended into the other realm."

"Nonsense," said Nero.

"Before that, he was seen alive by hundreds of people." For one instant Paul thought he had Nero's attention.

"This word *Christian*, where did it come from? Is it a play on words? I am told someone started calling you this in jest, mocking the word *Caesaer-ist*—those who are doubly loyal to Caesar—and thereby came up with the word *Christ-ist*."

Paul was frustrated. This was not what he had hoped. At this point Paul was coming to understand that, at best, he might be able to say only two or three more sentences. It was at this moment, Paul did a daring thing.

"Oh, great Caesar, the one true God has sent his Son, Jesus Christ, to the world to save men from their sins and bring them to full righteousness and holiness before God—the God before whom we all must stand."

Nero glared. "Dare you speak of your 'God' to a god?"

The magistrates, taking their cue, ordered Paul to silence. Nero managed a gruff laugh.

As he left to go, Nero said: "This city is full of too many religious fanatics." Just as he was about to disappear, he turned back. "What is your advice to me concerning this man?"

"Our advice had been to set him free, but it is yours to decide."

"Then set him free. What do I have to fear from the babblings of a religious fanatic?"

Nero disappeared, his words almost immediately becoming indistinct. But Paul did hear one sentence: "As to the garden, it will be the largest and most beautiful in the world. I am told it will be finished in two years, also the statue. But the palace . . ."

Paul's heart sank. He had stood before Nero, but he had failed in speaking to him of his testimony. Paul's only consolation was that the man he stood before was not totally sane.

"How dare you?" growled one of the magistrates. "Never have I seen such insolence. For this, you should have your head cut off! And it would be except Nero has set you free." With that, two soldiers grabbed Paul.

"Now out of here! Never let your face be seen in this place again. For if it is, you will surely *die.*"

The soldiers pushed Paul out to the street. Paul was almost literally thrown on the pavement. Then, in the street, a sheet of parchment was thrust into the hands of Priscilla. At that very moment, Paul heard singing. Not far away, awaiting him, stood virtually every Christian in Rome. Joyfully they rushed to his side.

"He is free!" exclaimed a tearful Priscilla. "Paul stood before Nero, and he is free!" There in the noisiest city on earth, no other sounds but the shouts of Christians could be heard.

That triumphant moment that day shone more than any other in the years to come. In retrospect, it could be argued that Paul's witness to Nero may have later been the cause of the torture and death of hundreds of believers.

Nero would grow in his madness. His ruthlessness, his depravity would cause him to become the greatest monster and buffoon in all human history.

Nero had but six years to live. So also Paul.

They would meet again. And shortly thereafter both would meet an ignominious death.

The very day Paul stood before Nero, Paul made a decision that would ensure his life on this earth for a few more years.

CHAPTER 16

Late that night the entire assembly in Rome met with Paul and Priscilla to hear the story of what happened to Paul when he was on trial. In all, there were about three hundred believers in the room. Half or more had been added since Paul arrived in Rome, most during the last year.

Paul and Priscilla together recounted their story. Their words were often interrupted by gales of laughter or shouts of praise. The meeting ended in a thunderous torrent of praise.

That same night Paul met with a group of men and women whose wisdom he trusted. Should he visit the churches in Galatia, Greece, and Asia Minor? Or should he remain in Rome for a while . . . or . . . ?

(Not until now had Paul allowed himself to think beyond the day that he would stand trial, for beyond that trial there was no tomorrow.)

That night the answer as to what Paul should do next became very clear.

Peter had once written a letter to Paul urging him *never* to return to Israel. There were spies scattered throughout the Gentile world waiting to report to the Daggermen the whereabouts of both Paul and Peter.

Further, in just four years Israel would revolt against Rome.

In six years the Roman armies would reconquer most of Israel. And in eight years Jerusalem would be destroyed.

At that moment, as Paul sat in Priscilla's house, Israel had reached the very edge of revolt. Clashes with the Romans were occurring almost daily. There was a growing conviction among Jewish *believers* everywhere that it was only a matter of time before the leaders of Israel would call upon the people to break from Rome and set up their own government.

In the midst of all this, the three men Israel most hated were Nero . . . and Peter and Paul.

If not Israel, and with spies everywhere, where should Paul go? For a moment silence filled the room.

"Many times you have mentioned going to Spain," observed Aristarchus. Several in the room immediately nodded their heads in agreement. "I believe it is time you fulfilled this hope."

Everyone, upon hearing Aristarchus's words, knew the decision had been made.

The next day Paul dispatched a number of men to spread the word to all of the assemblies that Paul was alive *and* that he had disappeared.

Paul's final day in Rome was spent with the Jewish leaders. Their meeting was in the synagogue itself. By that time perhaps a thousand Jews had returned to Rome. Ironically, it was far safer for a Jew to be in Rome than in Israel. The reason was simple: Nero's mistress, Poppaea, was a champion of the Jews. Nero, therefore, managed to make a distinction between the Jews in Israel and the Jews who lived in Rome.

While speaking in the newly opened synagogue that day, Paul made some inroads among the God-fearers and among the Jews.

As a result the assembly continued to grow, and the new Jewish additions fit right in with the ebullient Gentiles. The believers, Jew and Greek, continued to meet in Priscilla's home, though most of them lived in the Trastavere district. By the end of the year a strong three hundred were gathering.

Having finished speaking in the synagogue, Paul took passage on a small trading vessel that circumnavigated the Mediterranean by hovering close to the coast. Once the ship reached Spain, Paul disembarked at every town and village where the ship docked. He always went straight to the marketplace and proclaimed Christ.

That Paul had sailed west was a very tightly kept secret. As far as the world knew, Paul was no more.

The voyage to Spain and back added two more years to his journeys. Then one day he did return, and in haste.

What brought Paul back? The horrible death of one of his dearest friends on earth.

CHAPTER 17

It was the death of Aristarchus that brought Paul back from Spain.

Alas, dear reader, I, Gaius, must tell you that, from this point on, the story turns bloody. Please know I recount the next page in this saga with great sorrow, for these were the darkest days in the history of our faith. What started this horror?

Rome burned.

A fire swept the entire city. All but four districts were scorched.

The fire began on the night of July 18. In an hour it raged across most of the city, then burned for days. This event took place thirty-four years after Pentecost and six years before Jerusalem and the temple were leveled.

A rumor arose that Nero had started the fire because he needed space to build his palace. Another rumor followed: Nero had left Rome just before the fire and had watched it with glee, quoting passages of poetry telling of the fall of Troy . . . and doing so while playing on a lyre.

(Nero's home did *not* burn in the fire on that July night; neither did that of his friend Tigellimus.)

Were the two rumors true? No one knows. But Nero knew he needed a scapegoat. Although there were fewer than four hundred believers in the Roman assembly (in a city of over one million), Nero knew much about these strange ones. He also knew his palace alone would take up one-tenth of the entire city and that this did not sit well with Romans. That he was having a ninety-foot-high statue made of himself only added to the agitation.

Nero noted that of the fourteen districts of Rome, four districts were *not* damaged by the inferno, and two of those districts were where most of the Christians lived.

Nero began to plot. What he did not only sealed the fate of Paul and Peter but also that of Nero himself.

It had already galled Nero that some Christians were calling him the antithesis of Christ. Further, the Christians in his household were a bit too godly and pure for all that was going on in the palace. Once he heard a servant say that Claudius was all that Christ is not. Nero, in that mad mind of his, was jealous! He decided that he and Claudius were competitors, and *he* wanted to be the antithesis of this Christ!

So it was that Nero conjured up his fiendish plot. He would blame the "Christ-ists" for the fire, prove it, and then sentence them to death.

First he spread the rumor that this miserable sect had set the fire and that he had proof. After a few weeks of Rome's hearing this, Nero's soldiers—in one lightning stroke—jailed most of the Christians in Rome.

Eventually all of those captured were murdered at Nero's behest.

Since that day, we Christians have never known rest anywhere in the empire.

I must warn you that the words I am about to pen are heartbreaking, for I must tell you how the brothers and sisters in the assembly in Rome met their fate.

CHAPTER 18

More than two hundred believers were seized in the night and dragged to prison. Without a trial, they were sentenced to death.

Among those who were seized was our dear and beloved Aristarchus.

Thank God, Priscilla and Aquila were on their way to visit their beloved friends in Ephesus. Paul was in Spain. Had it not been so, all of them would have met certain death.

Nero divided his Christian captives into two groups. The first group would die at the mouths of wild dogs in the Circus Maximus. The others would be kept until Nero's garden was completed.

I, Gaius, find it very difficult to recount what happened next. And yet, if you are a follower of Christ, these are events that should not be forgotten.

Among the Christians put on display in the Circus Maximus many were disposed of by the sword. Others had bloody animal skins tied to their bodies. Then they were dragged into the Circus, where doors were opened and wild, hungry dogs were let loose on them. Applause swept the Circus as the dogs feasted on our brothers and sisters in Christ. Nero was ecstatic.

Although he had quelled the rumors concerning himself, that crime played a major role in Nero's doom. Everyone knew these people were innocent. Rome was beginning to learn to despise their twenty-four-year-old emperor. After all, he was still tearing down a large part of Rome just to build a garden nearly a mile long and a palace, called the Golden House, which seemed almost as large.

Sometime later, when Nero's garden was finished, in order to celebrate its completion, he invited the elite of Rome to a vast party that stretched across most of the garden. Nero then had the surviving Christian captives wrapped in cloth and soaked in oil. During the party, he had the Christians strung, heads down, on poles. Nero mounted a chariot, torch in hand and sped through the garden setting fire to our brothers and sisters. The fire illuminated the new garden. That night Nero's guests dined by the light of burning Christians.

Please note that most of the believers whose names are mentioned on the last page of the book of Romans died that same hideous evening! One who died in that holocaust was our beloved Aristarchus.

It was *this* that brought Paul home from Spain. And from the moment Paul returned he was a man who cared not whether he lived or died.

Nero had four years to live. Jerusalem had six years to exist. Those next six years would be among the bloodiest in all human history. And, as I noted earlier, virtually every one of the Twelve and all but one of the Eight died during those six years.

What happened shortly after this atrocity in Nero's garden is just as sorrowful.

CHAPTER 19

What happened next surprised even Nero.

Word traveled quickly throughout the empire that Nero was killing Christians.

Until that time most of the empire was not even aware of the existence of "Christ-ists." Those who were had only a vague idea that some sect of the Hebrew religion was growing, its followers being enthusiastic about their Jewish God.

Nero had signed no proclamation against Christians, nor did he banish them from Rome. His thought had simply been to remove blame from himself for the July 18 fire. Nonetheless, news of events in Rome was news for the world.

Suddenly an empire knew of the Christians, and, to find favor with the emperor, the local rulers, governors, and magistrates began searching their towns, cities, and provinces to see if there were assemblies among them. Rumors abounded. Persecution of our brothers and our sisters, both great and trivial, was taking place in virtually every province. Christians were suddenly living in terror.

As a result, some assemblies grew, some shrank.

Even Jews in Israel who had no particular liking of Christians understood the implication of their own future. They knew most people thought all Christians to be Jews. That meant the Jewish people now had one more mark against them. Hebrew people swallowed hard at the thought of Jewish believers and Gentile Christians dangling from poles while being burned alive.

Even Blastinius, I was told, found no joy in hearing this horrid news. Every Jew in Israel knew this would only make it harder for Israel to tolerate Rome's boot much longer. It also gave the fanatics in Israel more words to add to their denunciation of Rome. The call for revolt intensified.

The incident in the garden also stirred up the Twelve. They began telling all Jewish believers to move out of Israel *immediately*. Shortly thereafter, the Twelve also left Israel. This brings us to a whole new page in the history of our faith.

With the twelve Jewish apostles now leaving Israel and a mass influx of Jewish believers arriving in Gentile lands and joining themselves to Gentile assemblies, the question was this: Would the Jewish gospel and the practices of the Jewish assemblies prevail, or would the Gentile gospel and the Gentile expression of the church prevail?

Would it be a Christian faith and practice that looked like a synagogue, or a rousing, free Gentile expression that would come to the fore?

No matter which way it turned out, the answer would forever set the course of the faith. The two men who would most influence the direction of the assemblies were Peter and Paul—men not likely to be a unifying force between Jews and Gentiles.

There was a man out there struggling hard to locate Paul. This man had been sent by Peter. Peter's goal was to see to it that he and Paul might speak as one voice. The man who was trying to bring this to pass was a man not likely to fill this crucial role—at least not in Paul's eyes.

CHAPTER 20

John Mark's arrival in Nicopolis surprised Paul.

"Peter is considering writing a letter?" exclaimed Paul. "How could he possibly write a letter; he can't even read!"

"I'm teaching him," said Mark, with a grin.

"At his age?" replied an incredulous Paul.

That Peter was thinking of writing a letter to all the Jews fleeing Israel was even more surprising.

"There is much more to tell," continued Mark. "The Twelve have left Israel."

"Good! It is way *past* time for that! It has been nearly thirty-six years since Pentecost. Aren't the Twelve a little late fulfilling the Lord's prediction that they should go to the ends of the earth?" added Paul facetiously.

At that moment Peter was certain that virtually every believer in Israel had departed. He was certain the fulfillment of the Lord's words about the armies of the Gentiles surrounding Jerusalem was near.

Paul fully agreed with Peter's view.

"The Jews who flee to north Africa will find mostly Gentile assemblies, but these assemblies will have doors wide open to believing Jews," said Mark.

"The people in the assemblies in north Africa are about

equally balanced in the number of Jews and Gentiles in most cases," continued Mark, "yet their expression is definitely Gentile."

"So Gaius has said in a letter he has written to me," agreed Paul.

"If a Hebrew flees west to Bithynia or Byzantium, or flees east to Assyria, he just may find one of the Twelve. Most of the Twelve have moved east," continued Mark.

"A gracious gesture on their part," observed Paul, realizing that a western move would bring Jewish believers to assemblies wholly Gentile in nature.

Mark went on: "It is the Jewish believers who flee north who are of the greatest concern to Peter. He has stated that he believes you are just as concerned. Peter knows that, throughout your ministry, you have fought to keep peace and unity between the Jewish churches and the Gentile churches. In fact, Peter has said to everyone, 'Paul has been a hated man, a hunted man, a beaten man, a prisoner, and now a fugitive—all because he has fought to keep the Jewish and Gentile churches in oneness.'"

Paul's eyes filled with tears. "I was not aware anyone had noticed," he replied, his voice choked with emotion. "What does Peter propose?"

"Peter plans to write a letter to the Jews who flee north . . . to Galatia, to Cappadocia, to . . . "

"To all of Asia Minor?" asked Paul, a little surprised.

"Yes, Paul," replied Mark.

(The churches in Asia Minor are all Gentile churches. Asia Minor is a large area that begins just above Antioch, moving westward, and then northward extending to Troas, Ephesus, Bithynia, and Byzantium. On the northwest side, Asia Minor reaches almost to Greece. This, it turned out, is where most Jewish believers fled. As their second choice they fled to Greece.)

"Now tell me, *when* does Peter plan to write this letter?"

"As soon as I report back to him, but not before he knows if you are receptive to his plan."

Paul was about to reflect on the question, but Mark interrupted. "Peter has a suggestion to make. The Jewish exiles—their dispersal will be massive."

"I understand," answered Paul thoughtfully. "Jewish believers could overwhelm the Gentile churches in numbers, at least in some places. What does Peter propose?"

"This," answered Mark urgently. "Jewish believers are used to elders. Elders are a tradition among Hebrews that dates back all the way to Abraham. Jews *respect* elders! Peter notices, on the other hand, there are many Gentile churches that do not even have elders."

"Correct," said Paul, a bit of pride reflected in his answer. "For instance, there are a good number of churches on the island of Crete and not one elder in any of them. Scores of cities have assemblies, and yet there is not so much as one elder in any of those cities."

Mark blinked. "No elders in any assembly in any city on Crete?"

"And most of the ecclesiae in Asia Minor have none."

Mark paused. "No wonder Peter told me to *implore* you to appoint elders in *every* city in Asia Minor."

"Peter said that?" questioned Paul.

"Yes, he did. He hinted that you would be wise to make sure every assembly had elders because Jewish believers will soon be there among the Gentiles—and Jews understand eldership."

"Oh, I see!" answered Paul quickly. "Peter is correct. Jews *expect* elders; they will listen to them. On the other hand, Gentiles have no such tradition. Eldership means little or nothing to the Gentile believers. The entire assembly leads itself. As you know, the church in Antioch, as large as it is, has never had elders."

Mark blinked again.

Paul began to mull over Peter's question.

"If Peter is right about Gentile churches needing elders for the sake of incoming Jews, then I need to get letters off to Timothy and Titus. And it would be wise if those two letters arrived about the same time as Peter's letter to the fleeing Jews or maybe a little sooner."

"Excellent!" exclaimed Mark.

"Brother Mark, return to Peter, and tell him to get his letter out to Asia Minor immediately. There are already many believing Jews who live in Asia Minor, many who have fled there only recently, and more—many more—will pass through Asia Minor if Israel revolts against Rome. I believe that revolt will come . . . any day."

The conversation then changed direction. Paul began telling Mark of what had been happening to Christians in Rome, of the death of Aristarchus and the persecution of Gentile believers all over the empire. He also told of his return from Spain and of being hunted throughout the empire, forcing him to hide in Nicopolis. "We are not very popular, just as the Lord said," sighed Paul.

Mark began to tell what he had seen and heard of persecution in other lands. The two men were in tears as they spoke. They began to pray. They embraced. Tears fell copiously, and in that moment came a healing. It was the healing of a rift that had happened between these two men twenty years earlier.

"Mark, I have one question to ask before you go: What is Peter doing in Italy? The assembly in Rome is in hiding and in shambles. I have even heard rumors that many Roman believers have fled as far as the valleys of the Alps. Why is Peter in Italy?"

Mark threw back his head and laughed uproariously.

Paul was mystified.

"Well," returned Mark, "because you asked him to go there."

Paul sat up straight, thought for a moment, then began to laugh. "So I did. So I did."

Immediately thereafter, Mark departed for Italy and was soon sitting beside Peter and a scribe named Sylvanus.

The content of the letter Peter wrote was so close to Paul's gospel that it sounded as though Paul had written the letter himself.

A few months later three new letters began to circulate all over the Gentile world. One was from Peter and contained some very remarkable passages. So also did the two letters Paul wrote to Timothy and Titus.

There were no small results from these letters. They changed the course of history. In fact, these three letters changed *your* life.

After reading Peter's letter, a few of the Jews were heard to comment, "Paul has converted Peter to be a Gentile." One reader was even heard to say, "Did not Paul write this letter and sign Peter's name to it?"

I, Gaius, can only say of Peter's letter that Mark's time with Paul and Barnabas had a very profound effect on Mark, and this was reflected in the letter Peter wrote with Mark's help. Here are a few very interesting passages from Peter's letter:

This letter is from Peter, an apostle of Jesus Christ.

I am writing to God's chosen people who are living as foreigners in the lands of Pontus, Galatia, Cappadocia, the province of Asia, and Bithynia. God the Father chose you long ago, and the Spirit has made you holy. As a result, you have obeyed Jesus Christ and are cleansed by his blood.

May you have more and more of God's special favor and wonderful peace. . . .

Dear friends, don't be surprised at the fiery trials you are going through, as if something strange were happening to you.

Instead, be very glad—because these trials will

make you partners with Christ in his suffering, and afterward you will have the wonderful joy of sharing his glory when it is displayed to all the world. . . .

I have written this short letter to you with the help of [Silvanus] as, whom I consider a faithful brother. My purpose in writing is to encourage you and assure you that the grace of God is with you no matter what happens.

What pleased Paul the most about Peter's letter was a statement Peter made at the close of the letter. Peter, writing to Jews, called a Gentile church a *sister* church!

Your sister church here in Rome sends you greetings, and so does my son Mark.

At about this same time Paul sat down and wrote to Timothy. Please note that Timothy was a gray-headed, middle-aged man. (He still had the face of a youth.) More to the point, Timothy had lived his entire adult life *with* Paul. Yet, here was Paul telling Timothy the qualifications of an elder! Timothy *knew* the qualifications! Why, then, did Paul list them here?

It was not for Timothy but for the people in the churches all over Asia Minor who would read this letter. All these churches were in blissful ignorance. They didn't have elders! The same was true on the island of Crete. Titus had raised up churches all over Crete and not one of those churches had an elder!

After receiving Paul's letter, Timothy set out across Asia Minor selecting and ordaining elders. God's people needed to understand that Timothy knew what he was doing and that Paul had asked him to do so. Scores of Gentile churches had never seen or heard of elders. In every church Timothy visited, he read the letter Paul had written to him. In this way, not a single person challenged Timothy's right to choose elders and ordain them.

As you read Paul's letter to Timothy, note that he also made swift work of some of the problems Timothy faced in Asia Minor.

Here are Paul's words about elders. (Incidentally, almost any man in any church met these qualifications.)

It is a true saying that if someone wants to be an elder, he desires an honorable responsibility. For an elder must be a man whose life cannot be spoken against. He must be faithful to his wife. He must exhibit self-control, live wisely, and have a good reputation. He must enjoy having guests in his home and must be able to teach. He must not be a heavy drinker or be violent. He must be gentle, peace loving, and not one who loves money. He must manage his own family well, with children who respect and obey him. For if a man cannot manage his own household, how can he take care of God's church?

An elder must not be a new Christian, because he might be proud of being chosen so soon, and the Devil will use that pride to make him fall. Also, people outside the church must speak well of him so that he will not fall into the Devil's trap and be disgraced.

In the same way, deacons must be people who are respected and have integrity. They must not be heavy drinkers and must not be greedy for money. They must be committed to the revealed truths of the Christian faith and must live with a clear conscience. Before they are appointed as deacons, they should be given other responsibilities in the church as a test of their character and ability. If they do well, then they may serve as deacons. . . .

Do not listen to complaints against an elder unless there are two or three witnesses to accuse him.

Paul also wrote a letter to Titus, but that letter had far more a sense of urgency. There were many churches on Crete, one in each city, and Titus had *never* even introduced the idea of elders to the Cretans.

Here again, Paul tells Titus, who had been with him over twenty years, the qualifications of elders. Titus knew what elders were, but the believers on Crete did not know who they were nor their qualifications. Titus's task was to be sure there would be elders in the churches *before* a vast influx of Jewish believers arrived.

This letter is written to Titus, my true child in the faith that we share.

May God the Father and Christ Jesus our Savior give you grace and peace.

I left you on the island of Crete so you could complete our work there and appoint elders in each town as I instructed you. An elder must be well thought of for his good life. He must be faithful to his wife, and his children must be believers who are not wild or rebellious. An elder must live a blameless life because he is God's minister. He must not be arrogant or quick-tempered; he must not be a heavy drinker, violent, or greedy for money. He must enjoy having guests in his home and must love all that is good. He must live wisely and be fair. He must live a devout and disciplined life. He must have a strong and steadfast belief in the trustworthy message he was taught; then he will be able to encourage others with right teaching and show those who oppose it where they are wrong.

It is almost humorous that Paul told Titus about elders. Many years earlier Titus had spent weeks in Jerusalem living with the original elders.

When Paul wrote Timothy, he stated that there was a great possibility that fleeing Jews might come into Gentile churches and start talking about "endless genealogies" and many other things that very religious Jews wasted time on.

But Paul was even more specific about this nonsense that some very religious Jews might engage in when they joined an ecclesia on Crete. Paul was anticipating the result of a large influx of such people. At the advice of Peter, Paul was telling these new arrivals to accept the Gentile churches as they were and *not* to attempt to Judaize a Gentile church. Here are some very strong words Paul wrote. (You will see echoes of what happened to Gentile churches in Galatia at the hands of religious Jews as you read this passage.)

> For there are many who rebel against right teaching; they engage in useless talk and deceive people. This is especially true of those who insist on circumcision for salvation. They must be silenced. By their wrong teaching, they have already turned whole families away from the truth. Such teachers only want your money.

Titus told me later that he swallowed hard when he read "The Gentiles must stop listening to Jewish myths and to the commands of people who have turned their backs on the truth."

Titus swallowed hard again when he read an even more explicit passage—one similar to what Paul wrote to Timothy:

> Do not get involved in foolish discussions about spiritual pedigrees or in quarrels and fights about obedience to Jewish laws. These kinds of things are useless and a waste of time. If anyone is causing divisions among you, give a first and second warning. After that, have nothing more to do with that person. For people like that

have turned away from the truth. They are sinning, and they condemn themselves.

It was thirty-six years after Pentecost and four years before the fall of Jerusalem when Peter and Paul wrote those letters. Amazingly, the ink was hardly dry on the parchment when war broke out between Israel and Rome. As soon as Israel broke away from Rome, civil war began between several Jewish political parties. This was followed by a year of out-and-out insanity in Israel as Jews fought Jews over power. It has been stated that over twenty thousand Jews died in this civil war. Eventually though, this brother killing brother ended. The Hebrews were forced to focus on the Romans.

Paul, Nero, and Peter now had two years left to live. In the next two years—no, in the next *four* years—blood flowed thick and deep throughout the empire.

It now is my sad task to tell you of what befell the workers; that is, I must tell you how the Twelve and the Eight died. Walk with me as I recount those four awful years.

We go first to that year when Paul, Nero, and Peter died.

CHAPTER 22

Israel's revolt against Rome lasted two years. Then came Rome's preparation to reconquer Israel. This invasion of Israel took place thirty-eight years after Pentecost and two years before the destruction of Jerusalem.

Try to imagine sixty thousand Roman soldiers marching from Rome to Israel. The earth literally quaked under the soldiers' tramp. The army of Rome was commanded by a general named Flavius Vespasian.

At the time the Roman army departed for Israel, Nero was in Greece participating in the Olympics! Is it not mysterious that Nero was winning every event he entered? Even when Nero fell from his chariot, he was still announced the winner. He was so overcome with joy that he liberated all Greece from taxation. Shortly after that, the Greeks announced that all the games of Greece were to be played at one time so that Nero could enter every contest Greece had to offer. Amazingly, Nero won 1,808 contests. What Nero did not know was that the Praetorian Guard was making jokes about him—sure evidence that he would soon be dead.

In this same period not only did Israel revolt, but Gaul as well as Spain announced their independence from Rome. Nero should have taken note. He didn't.

In the meantime, Flavius Vespasian had prepared well for a distant war. First he had the seaports of Israel blocked. He then dispatched whole armies southward, some by sea, some by land—north and south of Israel. But most of all, Vespasian made a show of force. He marched his vast army through one province after another.

Thousands of soldiers marched to southern Italy, crossed to Greece, then marched the full breadth of Greece. From there the army sailed to Asia Minor. There this mighty war machine began a march down to Antioch in Syria. The world stood agog at the might of Rome.

Ironically, thousands of Jews were fleeing Israel, taking the same road north that this army was taking south. The Romans ignored the refugees; that is, unless one dared mock them. In that case, the offender was killed where he stood.

Truthfully, in virtually every place there was a sense of reverence as the people watched an endless line of troops descend on Israel's border. No one questioned the outcome.

While all this was taking place, Peter was hiding somewhere in Rome. Paul was secretly living in Nicopolis. Nero was on his way back to Rome, where he threw a triumphant welcome for himself. With him were his 1,808 trophies.

Rome was smart enough to give Nero a hero's welcome.

Once Vespasian's army entered Israel, virtually all of that nation fell to the Roman sword in a matter of months. Many towns and villages were completely empty when the army arrived. Israel as a Jewish nation was going out of existence.

At that very time, everywhere in the Diaspora, be it north or south, the Gentile churches were caring for fleeing Jewish believers. Gentile assemblies were being overwhelmed by large numbers of Jewish followers of Christ—just as Peter and Paul had expected. And always, there were copies of letters—Peter's letter to Asia Minor and Paul's letters to Timothy and Titus.

Israel had ceased to exist, but Jerusalem was another matter. Jerusalem would not surrender. That city, and an obscure fortress in the Judean desert called Masada, refused to consider surrendering to Rome. The Romans laid siege to Jerusalem—a siege that would last two years.

At that time Nero decided Paul was an enemy of Rome. Shortly thereafter Paul was arrested in Nicopolis. After he arrived in Rome and was tried, he was executed. So also was Peter.

(But I must lay aside the details of Paul's death for the moment.)

In the nations near Israel, a great reaction set in against all Jews. In just one day 10,000 Jews were slain in Damascus. In Caesarca, also in one day, 20,000 Hebrews were killed. When the army of Flavius Vespasian arrived at Jerusalem's gates, some 650,000 Jews swarmed into Jerusalem to defend the Holy City and await the Messiah.

Shortly thereafter the Praetorian Guard announced to Nero that they would no longer protect him. The Senate, hearing this, decreed his death. Nero then fled some four miles to a cellar, where he thrust a dagger through his throat, declaring, "Oh, what an artist in me dies!"

Word came to Vespasian that Nero had died. He immediately turned part of his army over to his thirty-three-year-old son, Flavius Titus. Taking part of his army with him, Vespasian marched back toward Rome. Flavius Titus continued the siege of Jerusalem. Starvation soon set in. Those who dared to try to slip outside Jerusalem were crucified. The Romans crucified so many people they ran out of wood since there was not a single tree left in all Israel. Inside the city, death by starvation was rampant. One day 116,000 corpses were thrown out over the wall, all dead from lack of food.

When Flavius Titus took over part of Jerusalem, he offered liberal surrender conditions to the Jews. They refused. We are told that shortly after that more than 300,000 Jews were slain by the Roman army. (One of those who died was Blastinius). Another 97,000 refugees were captured and taken as slaves.

The Jewish historian Josephus, who recently wrote of this war, states that 1,197,000 Jews died in this war.

In the meantime Vespasian decided on a leisurely march back to Rome. In the interval of that march, three new emperors rose and fell, all in a little over one year.

Vespasian then entered Rome and shortly thereafter was crowned emperor. One of the first things Vespasian did was to bring down the ninety-foot statue of Nero. Then he destroyed the garden and Nero's palace. Using a play on words and thereby creating a new Latin word, Vespasian declared: "There will be no Colossus, but I build for the people a new stadium . . . a *Coliseum.*"

On the site of the palace, Vespasian had a stadium built that would seat fifty thousand people. It was built by ten thousand Jewish slaves who were captured in the fall of Jerusalem. The Coliseum took ten years to complete. So ended Nero's era.

Now, before we speak further of Paul's death, I feel I must tell you how each of the Twelve met his death. And not only how the Twelve died but also how the Eight died.

CHAPTER 23

Hebrews
written
by
Barnabas

Just before Israel fell, Barnabas, serving his Lord on the island of Cypress and watching the Jewish people scatter across the empire, sensed the need of a letter to all of these Jews fleeing into the Gentile world. The Hebrews had always seen their law, their prophets, their heroes as being above and beyond all others. They could not think in terms of God having sent one greater than the prophets or greater than Moses. Jesus was greater than all who had come before. It was a Jewish tradition that when God did something new, it was always chronicled in writing!

Yes, an epistle to the Diaspora was needed. Barnabas decided to write it. The theme: Jesus Christ was superior to all else God ever did among the Hebrews.

When Barnabas sat down to write that book, he took upon himself the mantle of a Jewish prophet. Unwittingly, Barnabas, in writing this magnificent letter, also wrote a short but beautiful history of the Hebrew nation that greatly aided the Gentile Christians in understanding a people about whom they knew so little. Barnabas's letter turned out to be a book about Christ to the Jews as well as a book telling Gentiles about Jesus and Jewish history.

Long ago God spoke many times and in many ways to our ancestors through the prophets. But now in these final days, he has spoken to us through his Son. God promised everything to the Son as an inheritance, and through the Son he made the universe and everything in it. The Son reflects God's own glory, and everything about him represents God exactly. (He sustains the universe by the mighty power of his command. After he died to cleanse us from the stain of sin, he sat down in the place of honor at the right hand of the majestic God of heaven. . . .

So we must listen very carefully to the truth we have heard, or we may drift away from it. . . .

What we do see is Jesus, who "for a little while was made lower than the angels" and now is "crowned with glory and honor" because he suffered death for us. Yes, by God's grace, Jesus tasted death for everyone in all the world. And it was only right that God—who made everything and for whom everything was made—should bring his many children into glory. Through the suffering of Jesus, God made him a perfect leader, one fit to bring them into their salvation.

So now Jesus and the ones he makes holy have the same Father. That is why Jesus is not ashamed to call them his brothers and sisters. . . .

So Christ has now become the High Priest over all the good things that have come. He has entered that great, perfect sanctuary in heaven, not made by human hands and not part of this created world. . . .

Under the old system, the blood of goats and bulls and the ashes of a young cow could cleanse people's bodies from ritual defilement. Just think how much more the blood of Christ will purify our hearts from deeds that lead to death so that we can worship the living God. For by the power of the eternal Spirit, Christ offered himself to God as a perfect sacrifice for our sins. That is why he is the one who mediates the new covenant between God and people, so that all who are invited can receive the eternal inheritance God has promised them. For Christ died to set them free from the penalty of the sins they had committed under that first covenant. . . .

Now when sins have been forgiven, there is no need to offer any more sacrifices.

And so, dear brothers and sisters, we can boldly enter heaven's Most Holy Place because of the blood of Jesus. This is the new, life-giving way that Christ has opened up for us through the sacred curtain, by means of his death for us. . . .

Do not throw away this confident trust in the Lord, no matter what happens. Remember the great reward it brings you! Patient endurance is what you need now, so you will continue to do God's will. Then you will receive all that he has promised. . . .

What is faith? It is the confident assurance that what we hope for is going to happen. It is the evidence of things we cannot yet see. God gave his approval to people in days of old because of their faith.

By faith we understand that the entire universe was formed at God's command, that what we now see did not come from anything that can be seen.

It was by faith that Abel brought a more acceptable offering to God than Cain did. . . .

It was by faith that Enoch was taken up to heaven without dying. . . .

It was by faith that Noah built an ark. . . .

It was by faith that Abraham obeyed when God called him to leave home and go to another land. . . .

It was by faith that Sarah together with Abraham was able to have a child. . . .

All these faithful ones died without receiving what

God had promised them, but they saw it all from a distance and welcomed the promises of God. They agreed that they were no more than foreigners and nomads here on earth. . . .

Well, how much more do I need to say? It would take too long to recount the stories of the faith of Gideon, Barak, Samson, Jephthah, David, Samuel, and all the prophets. By faith these people overthrew kingdoms, ruled with justice, and received what God had promised them. . . .

But others trusted God and were tortured, preferring to die rather than turn from God and be free. They placed their hope in the resurrection to a better life. . . .

Jesus Christ is the same yesterday, today, and forever. So do not be attracted by strange, new ideas. Your spiritual strength comes from God's special favor, not from ceremonial rules about food, which don't help those who follow them. . . .

For this world is not our home; we are looking forward to our city in heaven, which is yet to come.

Just as Barnabas finished this letter, Timothy was released from prison. Days afterward, Israel fell to the army of Flavius Titus.

Peter wrote a letter just before he was crucified in Rome. He, himself, actually penned this letter, so it is a little difficult to read!

Just after Barnabas's book to the Hebrews began to be copied and sent throughout the empire, Barnabas met his death on his beloved island of Cypress. From the time of the fire in Rome, on through the fall of Jerusalem and the death of Flavius Domitian, a period of thirty-two years, the Lord's churches knew no rest from persecution. During this same time, all of the Twelve except one were killed. So also seven of the Eight, Paul's colaborers. Only I remain alive.

From the Day of Pentecost until the death of the emperor Domitian covers a period of sixty-six years.

How did these men die? I can only tell you of what I, Gaius, now an old man, have heard.

Andrew traveled to, and perished in, Byzantium. Before his death, he made his way to Patros, below Corinth. The magistrate, Aigatis, had Andrew arrested and crucified. He hung for three days before he died.

I am told that Philip went west to the land of the Franks. Later he returned to Asia Minor. Remarkably, he died just sixteen miles from Epaphras's home in Hierapolis.

Of the death of Bartholomew I know nothing for sure. There is only a rumor that he was flayed alive in Armenia.

Of Thomas we know much. He went forth to the east, beyond all known maps, to a land sometimes called "far India," which is a place far, far beyond even Assyria. We are told his tomb is in Mylapore on the coast of a place called Charomandel. Of the manner of his death, I know nothing except he died for preaching Christ.

Of Matthew, we know only that he died in Egypt.

Thaddeus (that is Jude) traveled to Syria and perhaps Persia. We only know he was martyred somewhere in Syria—perhaps in Edessa.

Simon the Zealot died somewhere in Persia, sawn asunder for preaching the gospel in that land.

Of Matthias, who took the place of Judas Iscariot, we only have the rumor that he traveled to Mesopotamia. Nothing is known of the details of his death.

John Mark, a man faithful in his colaboring with Barnabas and Peter, and later a strong and faithful coworker with Paul, made his way to Alexandria, Egypt. There, I am told, his Gospel of Mark was translated into Egyptian. It is reported that he was torn asunder by horses.

As I noted, Barnabas died in Salamis, Cypress. At some

point in his ministry there, a heathen mob stoned him, then tied a rope around his neck and dragged him through the streets until he was dead.

John is alive, exiled on a tiny island in the Mediterranean, not far from Ephesus.

Of Luke, I know only that he died in Bithynia at a very old age.

So much sorrow. Such nobility in death.

And what of the Eight?

Yes, what of the Eight?

Timothy was arrested not long after Paul's death. It seems the whole kingdom of God on earth prayed for his release. Shortly after he was released from prison, Timothy was bludgeoned to death on the streets of Ephesus.

Titus lived out his life preaching Christ on the islands of the Mediterranean and met his end on the island of Crete.

Aristarchus, as you know, was burned alive in the garden of Nero.

Sopater met his end in Berea.

The beloved Secundus was killed somewhere on the frontiers of western Europe.

Trophimus was with Paul in Miletus at the time soldiers were seeking Paul. Trophimus recovered from his illness and made a swift return to Rome. Later he came back to the assembly in Miletus, where soon thereafter he was put to death.

Tychicus was arrested somewhere in Asia Minor, brought to Ephesus, and killed in the arena.

And Epaphras? He ministered long and faithfully in eastern Asia Minor. He was in Colosse at the time of his martyrdom. He died as he lived, facing death steadfastly and with praise to his Lord until the last breath.

So many have asked me of the fate of Onesimus. Philemon set him free! Did he really have any other choice? Until this day Philemon's letter is still passed about everywhere and is always met with smiles and chuckles at Paul's sagacity.

As I write, the reign of Flavius Vespasian, Flavius Titus, and the horrid Flavius Domitian have all ended. Domitian was assassinated sixty-six years after Pentecost.

A man named Nerva now sits on the throne of Rome. Today, as I come to the end of my life, I note that it has been seventy years since Pentecost. Thirty years have passed since the fall of Jerusalem.

Only I, Gaius, of the Eight am alive. John is the sole survivor of the Twelve.

Bear with me now as I return to that day just two years before Jerusalem fell (and thirty-eight years after Pentecost), when Paul was executed.

I, Gaius, *must* recount to you this last page in Paul's life, for I was with him on the day of his coronation: I saw Paul die. I know of your love for him and that you will want to know of his last hours on earth.

Return with me, then, to that most remarkable hour.

CHAPTER 25

Paul was arrested in Nicopolis, Greece, and taken directly to Rome.

Most of the original forty people whom Paul sent to Rome to raise up the assembly there had been killed by Nero. The rest of the believers were in hiding. (At that time, as I noted earlier, Priscilla and Aquila had gone to visit Ephesus.)

Luke and a few others still dared to remain in Rome, mostly for Paul's sake. Among those who were with Paul were Eubulus, Pudens, Linus, and Claudia. Beyond that, perhaps a dozen believers still dared remain in Rome, meeting always in secret.

While Paul waited for a hearing, Alexander the copper-smith of Ephesus wrote letters and sent other people's letters to the judges with all sorts of charges against Paul.

To let God's people know of his dire situation, Paul sent a Roman brother named Crescens to Galatia. Titus was sent to the new assemblies in Dalmatia. To every area of the empire Paul sent someone to inform the churches of his situation. A number of Christians, especially in Asia Minor, sent messengers to Rome to stand with Paul.

Just after his first hearing, Paul wrote a second letter to Timothy. He then hurriedly dispatched the ever-faithful

Tychicus to Ephesus to find Timothy and give him the letter. Tychicus found Timothy and took his place in Ephesus so Timothy could go immediately to Rome.

Paul knew what awaited him at the second hearing: He would be condemned to die. The only good news was that the second hearing would not take place for six months. Winter lay between the first hearing and the second.

As soon as that first hearing ended, Demas, sent by the church in Thessalonica to care for Paul, panicked and fled the city. Others, sent from Asia Minor to stand by Paul, ceased visiting Paul in the Tullian Prison.

I must admit that this particular prison, the Tullian, would terrify any visitor. It was well known that, from time to time, visitors were sometimes arrested *in* the prison, never to be seen again.

As his second letter to Timothy indicated, Paul felt betrayed.

Many had said they would be there with Paul at the first hearing, regardless of the circumstances. But so many people were arrested the previous week that no one dared be at Paul's side.

Luke, protected by Roman law because he was a physician, was the only person standing beside Paul that day.

The judges treated Paul terribly at the first hearing. Seeing clearly that they meant to sentence him to death at the second hearing, Paul unleashed the gospel in that courtroom, calling all present to believe in Christ. This display of audacity set well with no one.

It was when Paul returned to his cell that he wrote that second epistle to Timothy. Although Paul urged Timothy to find Mark, leave Ephesus, and hurry to Rome, he still wrote the letter knowing he might never see Timothy again.

Here are a few lines from Paul's second letter to his "son in the faith":

This letter is from Paul, an apostle of Christ Jesus by God's will, sent out to tell others about the life he has promised through faith in Christ Jesus.

It is written to Timothy, my dear son.

May God our Father and Christ Jesus our Lord give you grace, mercy, and peace.

Timothy, I thank God for you. He is the God I serve with a clear conscience, just as my ancestors did. Night and day I constantly remember you in my prayers. I long to see you again, for I remember your tears as we parted. And I will be filled with joy when we are together again. . . .

As you know, all the Christians who came here from the province of Asia have deserted me; even Phygelus and Hermogenes are gone. May the Lord show special kindness to Onesiphorus and all his family because he often visited and encouraged me. He was never ashamed of me because I was in prison. When he came to Rome, he searched everywhere until he found me. . . .

As for me, my life has already been poured out as an offering to God. The time of my death is near. . . .

Please come as soon as you can. . . .

The first time I was brought before the judge, no one was with me. Everyone had abandoned me. I hope it will not be counted against them. But the Lord stood with me and gave me strength, that I might preach the Good News in all its fullness for all the Gentiles to hear. And he saved me from certain death. Yes, and the Lord will deliver me from every evil attack and will bring me safely to his heavenly Kingdom. To God be the glory forever and ever. Amen.

Give my greetings to Priscilla and Aquila and those living at the household of Onesiphorus. Erastus stayed at Corinth, and I left Trophimus sick at Miletus.

Hurry so you can get here before winter. Eubulus sends you greetings, and so do Pudens, Linus, Claudia, and all the brothers and sisters.

Timothy's heart broke when he read Paul's letter, discovering that the Christians who went to Rome to be with Paul at the hearing had run when personal danger arose. Further, Timothy could not bear the thought that this man of God would die believing he was forsaken. Timothy determined that Paul would find out the truth before he died.

Timothy immediately had scores of Paul's letter copied and sent *everywhere*. He attached a brief note of his own: "Everyone, everywhere, find the men who are still alive whom Paul trained at Ephesus. Tell them to go immediately to Rome. Help those men get to Rome, at any cost. Present them with enough money to get to Rome the *fastest* possible way."

And the churches responded.

A few days later, with Mark at his side, Timothy set out for Rome. (Remember, all this was taking place just two years before Jerusalem fell.)

I, Gaius, having heard that Paul had been arrested again, had already determined to go to Rome. I was in Galatia at the time Timothy's urgent note reached the four churches in Galatia. The Galatians gave me a gift more than adequate to reach Rome, then sent me on my way. I moved as fast as a man could travel. The Galatians more or less demanded: "Spare no expense. Be there at Paul's side before he dies. Send our love."

As a result I found myself traveling by horse, caravan, ferry, and ship. My determination to arrive in Rome before Paul's last winter was as strong as the determination of the Galatians to help me get there.

From Dalmatia came Titus in similar fashion. Secundus came from Malta. Trophimus, now recovered from his illness at Miletus, in the company of Sopater, also moved quickly toward Rome.

Tychicus alone did not come. Obeying Paul, he stayed in Ephesus to deal with a crisis among some of the Ephesian elders who had not yet learned to become *only brothers* in the church there.

As Paul requested in his letter, Timothy did bring the cloak Paul left in Troas, along with even much better and warmer clothing. And yes, Carpus sent a messenger with Timothy to Rome, the messenger carrying Paul's books and papers! Priscilla, in Ephesus, sent a very touching letter to Paul. Her letter was probably the last that Paul read.

All of us arrived within a week of one another. We immediately went into hiding in the insula of a brother named Eubulus.

It took weeks for even one of us to get permission to enter the Tullian Prison (also called the Gemonium Keep). This prison had many levels of cells in it. Paul, a Roman, was not confined to the hideous Mamertine cells.

Gradually each of us did manage to have a few brief moments with Paul. He was astonished at our coming and was comforted by the news we brought from the churches. Nonetheless, we hardly had time to do more than greet him. Luke alone was given time to be with Paul. We plied Luke with every piece of information we could concerning the well-being of the assemblies, so that Luke, in turn, could pass that information on to Paul.

Paul was stunned—and elated—in hearing that the Gentile expression of the church was now in triumph and that the Jewish believers, fleeing Israel, were joining in with the boisterous Gentiles in their free-flowing meetings.

"Thanks to Peter and his wonderful letter," Paul stated emphatically.

"Perhaps your letter to Timothy and the one to Titus helped, too," added Luke.

Winter came and passed.

Spring was everywhere around us when Paul's second hearing took place. On that fateful day, about fifty brave souls stood at the front of the council door waiting for Paul's arrival. When Paul did arrive at the judicial building, he was surrounded by dour Roman guards.

As he passed us we shouted our lungs out, knowing full well we risked being run through by Roman blades. Paul's only outward acknowledgment of our presence was to raise one shackled hand. It was enough, though, to bring forth a full-throated crescendo of praise.

As might be expected, one soldier broke rank and started at us with his sword. We instantly scattered. He cursed us and then rejoined his band. Just as quickly we reassembled, and even as Paul disappeared beyond the bronze doors, we burst into singing.

Silence ensued. We *knew* what the verdict would be. What we did not know was where and when Paul would be executed. That afternoon we learned.

Paul would be marched outside the city gate onto the Ostian Way. The place to which he was to be led is called Aquae Salviae. We were warned not to attempt to interfere with the execution or to even go near Paul or we would surely be killed.

There were seven men who slept not a moment that night—Timothy, Titus, Trophimus, Sopater, Secundus, Mark, and I. One thought only was on all our minds: Do we risk all of us dying, just to be near Paul as he is executed?

About midnight Eubulus came into the room where we all were staying. He announced, "Someone has arrived. He says he is one of you. He comes from Philippi."

One of us, I wondered. *Who?*

At that moment Epaphras filled the doorway. We grabbed him, hugged him, and then together we cried like children. In that plain, straightforward manner of Epaphras, he resolved our dilemma.

"I have come to be with Paul, and if it is to be, to die with him."

Immediately we all left the room and made our way straight to the Ostian Gate, there to await a band of Roman soldiers—and a Jew of small stature named Paul.

Just before dawn, above the din of the cattle being taken out of the city, we heard the soldiers coming.

As they slowly pushed open the gate, one of the soldiers saw us. "By the gods, if any one of you utters so much as one word we will slaughter you all."

Then came Paul, hardly visible in the dim light. Not one word was spoken; nonetheless, Paul knew we were there.

For our sake he was deliberately ignoring us. But there was a pride, a dignity in his step we had never seen before. He was proud of us, and he was showing us how to die!

We wanted so much to scream but dared not. For a moment Secundus ran forward but was stopped short when a guard drew his sword and brandished it angrily. Secundus retreated.

On we walked. And on we wept, aching to say something.

The guards approved the chosen site. Our tears began to flow like silent rivers.

The soldiers unshackled Paul. He raised his eyes to the heavens. He was going to say something to the Lord he was about to see face-to-face when Secundus broke ranks. He began, of all things, to cheer! He quoted some of Paul's last words, written in that second letter to Timothy.

"Brother Paul, you have fought the good fight. You . . ." Secundus stammered; he could not find his words.

Epaphras did. "You have finished the race. And you, Paul, have won that race!"

Timothy took up the words. "You have remained faithful."

"The prize, Brother Paul, the prize. You have won the prize!" shouted a tearful Trophimus.

"The crown is yours," I shouted, not giving a fig if they killed me on the spot.

Titus broke in. "You won, Paul. All across Asia Minor, you have won! And now, go to meet your Lord, and ours, in triumph!"

Then we all began to shout as one, our words mingling together in a flood of exhortations. "Now, in glory, meet your Lord. He awaits you. The crown awaits you."

"Paul, we will meet you soon. We will be there."

"Paul, we will be faithful."

"We will carry on. We will continue the fight. We will fight the good fight . . . as did you."

"We will take your place. We will move on to the ends of the earth, Paul! To the ends of the earth!"

"We will follow the example you have left us. We will pass that example on to a new generation."

"We will work with our hands."

Paul raised his face and his hands to the sky.

"We will owe no man anything but love."

"We will be Paul to all the saints—loving them, comforting them."

"We will pour out our lives as a drink offering to our brothers and sisters."

Then, as one, we cried out: "We will carry on!"

The morning sun caught the blade of the sword as it glistened in the sky. One mighty shout of praise by Paul . . . and then all things grew silent. Nothing moved. Not even the soldiers.

And within my heart, or from heaven's gates, I heard these words:

"The torch! Take the torch! Be keepers of the flame!"

If you enjoyed this series, you may enjoy The Chronicles of the Door series. While different in nature, this series follows biblical stories from the Creation to the return of Christ in five inspirational volumes.

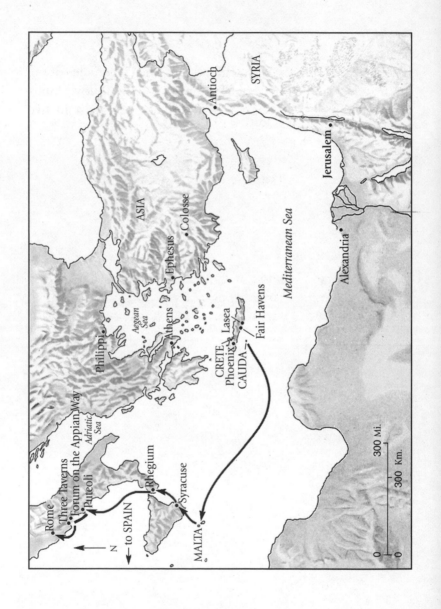

ABOUT THE AUTHOR

The author may be reached at:
Destiny Ministries
P. O. Box 3317
Jacksonville, FL 32206
destinymin@juno.com

For a free copy of a book by Gene Edwards that summarizes The First Century Diaries series, please write to the above address. You may also phone in your request at (904) 598-2347.